ALLIES OF THE NIGHT

THE SAGA OF DARREN SHAN
BOOK 8

Other titles by
DARREN SHAN

THE SAGA OF DARREN SHAN

THE DEMONATA

*Also available on audio

DARREN SHAN

ALLIES OF THE NIGHT

THE SAGA OF DARREN SHAN
BOOK 8

HarperCollins *Children's Books*

Hunt for Darren Shan on the web at
www.darrenshan.com

First published in Great Britain by HarperCollins *Children's Books* 2002
This edition published 2009
HarperCollins*Children'sBooks* is a division of HarperCollins*Publishers* Ltd,
1 London Bridge Street
London SE1 9GF

The HarperCollins website address is:
www.harpercollins.co.uk

5

ISBN-13   978 0 00 793900 8

Printed and bound by
CPI Group (UK) Ltd, Croydon, CR0 4YY

Mixed Sources
Product group from well-managed
forests and other controlled sources
www.fsc.org Cert no. SW-COC-1806
© 1996 Forest Stewardship Council
FSC

FSC is a non-profit international organisation established to promote the
responsible management of the world's forests. Products carrying the FSC
label are independently certified to assure consumers that they come
from forests that are managed to meet the social, economic and
ecological needs of present and future generations.

Find out more about HarperCollins and the environment at
www.harpercollins.co.uk/green

PROLOGUE

IT WAS an age of war. After six hundred years of peace, the vampires and vampaneze had taken up arms against each other in a brutal, bloody battle to the death. The War of the Scars began with the coming of the Lord of the Vampaneze. He was destined to lead his people to total, all-conquering victory — unless killed before he was fully blooded.

According to the mysterious and powerful Mr Tiny, only three vampires stood a chance of stopping the Vampaneze Lord. They were the Prince, Vancha March; the one-time General, Larten Crepsley; and a half-vampire, me — Darren Shan.

It was predicted by Mr Tiny that our path would cross four times with that of the Vampaneze Lord, and each time the destiny of the vampires would be ours for the making. If we killed him, we'd win the War of the Scars. If not, the vampaneze would cruise to savage victory and wipe our entire clan from the face of the earth.

Mr Tiny said we couldn't call upon other vampires for help during the quest, but we could accept the aid of non-vampires. Thus, when Mr Crepsley and me left Vampire Mountain (Vancha joined us later), the only one to come with us was Harkat Mulds, a stunted, grey-skinned Little Person.

Leaving the Mountain – our home for six years – we headed for the cave of Lady Evanna, a witch of great power. She could see into the future but would only reveal this much to us — if we failed to kill the Lord of the Vampaneze, by the end of our quest, two of us would be dead.

Later on, we linked up with the Cirque Du Freak, where I'd lived with Mr Crepsley when I originally became his assistant. Evanna travelled with us. At the Cirque, we ran into a group of vampaneze. A short fight ensued, during which most of the vampaneze were killed. Two escaped — a full-vampaneze by the name of Gannen Harst, and his servant, who we later learnt was the Lord of the Vampaneze, in disguise.

We were sickened when Evanna revealed the true identity of Gannen Harst's servant, but Vancha was especially miserable, because he had let them escape — Gannen Harst was Vancha's brother, and Vancha had let him go without challenging him, unaware that his brother was prime protector of the Vampaneze Lord.

But there was no time to sit around feeling sorry for ourselves. We still had three chances to find and kill our deadly foe, so our quest continued. Putting the lost chance behind us, we sharpened our blades, parted company with Evanna and our friends in the Cirque Du Freak, and took to the road again, more determined than ever to succeed...

CHAPTER ONE

YOUR DAILY POST, SEPTEMBER 15
BLOODY NIGHTS OF DEATH!!!

This once-sleepy city is under siege. In the space of six short months eleven people have been brutally murdered, their bodies drained of blood and dumped in various public places. Many more have vanished into the shadows of the night and might be lying beneath the streets, their lifeless bodies decomposing in the lonely dark.

Officials cannot account for the gruesome killing spree. They do not believe the murders to be the work of one man, but nor have they been able to link the crimes to any known criminals. In the largest single police operation in the city's history, most local gangs have been broken up, religious cult leaders arrested and the doors of secret orders and brotherhoods smashed down ... to no effect at all!

CUSTOMARY BLUNTNESS

Chief Inspector of police, Alice Burgess, when queried about the lack of results, responded with her own brand of customary bluntness. "We've been working like dogs," she snapped. "Everyone's on unpaid overtime. Nobody's shirking responsibility. We're patrolling the streets in force, arresting anyone who even *looks* suspicious. We've initiated a 7 pm curfew for children, and have advised adults to remain indoors too. If you find someone who can do a better job, give me a call and I'll gladly step aside."

Comforting words — but nobody here is taking comfort from them. The people of this city are tired of promises and pledges. Nobody doubts the honest, hard-working efforts of the local police – or the army who have been called in to assist in the operation – but faith in their ability to bring an end to the crisis has hit an all-time low. Many are moving out of the city, staying with relatives or in hotels, until the killings cease.

"I have kids," Michael Corbett, the forty-six-year-old owner of a second-hand bookshop told us. "Running away doesn't make me feel proud, and it'll ruin my business, but the lives of my wife and children come first. The police can do no more now than they did thirteen years ago. We've just got to wait for this to blow over, like it did before. When it does, I'll return. In the mean time, I think anyone who stays is crazy."

HISTORY OF DEATH

When Mr Corbett spoke of the past, he was referring to a time, nearly thirteen years ago, when horror similarly visited this city. On that occasion, nine bodies were discovered by a pair of teenagers, butchered and drained as the recent eleven victims have been.

But those bodies were carefully hidden, and only unearthed long after death had occurred. Today's murderers – rather, *tonight's*, since each victim has been taken after sunset – are not bothering to hide the evidence of their foul deeds. It's as though they are proud of their cruelty, leaving the bodies where they know they will be found.

Many locals believe the city is cursed and has a history of death. "I've been expecting these killings for fifty years," said Dr Kevin Beisty, a local historian and expert on the occult. "Vampires visited here more than one hundred and fifty years ago, and the thing about vampires is, once they find a place they like — they always come back!"

DEMONS OF THE NIGHT

Vampires. If Dr Beisty's was the only voice crying out against demons of the night, he could be dismissed as a crank. But many other people believe that we are suffering at the hands of vampires. They point to the fact that the attacks always occur at night, that the bodies have been drained of blood – seemingly without the aid of medical equipment – and, most tellingly, that although three of the victims were photographed by hidden security cameras when they were abducted, their attackers' faces *did not show up on film*!!

Chief Inspector Alice Burgess is dismissive of the vampire theory. "You think Count Dracula's on the rampage?" she laughed contemptuously. "Don't be ridiculous! This is the twenty-first century. Warped, sick humans are behind all this. Don't waste my time blaming bogeymen!"

When pushed, the Chief Inspector had this to add: "I don't believe in vampires, and I don't want idiots like you filling people's heads with such nonsense. But I'll tell you this: I'll do whatever it takes to stop these savages. If that means driving a stake through some madman's chest because he believes he's a vampire, I'll do it, even if it costs me my job and freedom. Nobody's walking away from this on an insanity plea. There's only one way to pay back the deaths of eleven good men and women — *extermination*!

"And I'll do it," Chief Inspector Burgess vowed, a fiery gleam in her pale eyes which would have done Professor Van Helsing proud. "Even if I have to track them to Transylvania and back. There'll be no escaping the sword of justice, be they humans or vampires.

"Tell your readers that I'll get their tormentors. They can bet on that. They can bet their *lives*..."

* * *

MR CREPSLEY pushed the manhole cover up and out of the way, while Harkat and me waited in the darkness below. After checking the street for signs of life, he whispered, "All clear," and we followed him up the ladder and out into fresh air.

"I hate those bloody tunnels," I groaned, slipping off my shoes, which were soaked through with water, mud and other things I didn't want to think about. I'd have to wash them out in the sink when we got back to the hotel and leave them on top of a radiator to dry, as I'd been doing at the end of every night for the past three months.

"I despise them too," Mr Crepsley agreed, gently prying the remains of a dead rat from the folds of his long red cloak.

"They're not so bad," Harkat chuckled. It was OK for him — he had no nose or sense of smell!

"At least the rain has held off," Mr Crepsley said.

"Give it another month," I replied sourly. "We'll be wading up to our hips down there by mid-October."

"We will have located and dealt with the vampaneze by then," Mr Crepsley said, without conviction.

"That's what you said two months ago," I reminded him.

"And last month," Harkat added.

"You wish to call off the search and leave these people to the vampaneze?" Mr Crepsley asked quietly.

Harkat and me looked at each other, then shook our heads. "Of course not," I sighed. "We're just tired and cranky. Let's get back to the hotel, dry ourselves off and get

15

something warm to eat. We'll be fine after a good day's sleep."

Finding a nearby fire escape, we climbed to the roof of the building and set off across the skylight of the city, where there were no police or soldiers.

Six months had passed since the Lord of the Vampaneze escaped. Vancha had gone to Vampire Mountain to tell the Princes and Generals the news, and had not yet returned. For the first three months Mr Crepsley, Harkat and me had roamed without purpose, letting our feet take us where they wished. Then word reached us of the terror in Mr Crepsley's home city — people were being killed, their bodies drained of blood. Reports claimed vampires were to blame, but we knew better. Rumours had previously reached us of a vampaneze presence in the city, and this was all the confirmation we needed.

Mr Crepsley cared for these people. Those he'd known when he lived here as a human were long since dead and buried, but he looked upon their grandchildren and great-grandchildren as his spiritual kin. Thirteen years earlier, when a mad vampaneze by the name of Murlough was savaging the city, Mr Crepsley returned – with me and Evra Von, a snake-boy from the Cirque Du Freak – to stop him. Now that history was repeating itself, he felt compelled to intervene again.

"But maybe I should ignore my feelings," he'd mused three months earlier, as we discussed the situation. "We must focus on the hunt for the Vampaneze Lord. It would be wrong of me to drag us away from our quest."

"Not so," I'd disagreed. "Mr Tiny told us we'd have to follow our hearts if we were to find the Vampaneze Lord. Your heart's drawing you home, and my heart says I should stick by you. I think we should go."

Harkat Mulds, a grey-skinned Little Person who'd learned to talk, agreed, so we set off for the city where Mr Crepsley had been born, to evaluate the situation and help if we could. When we arrived, we soon found ourselves in the middle of a perplexing mystery. Vampaneze were definitely living here – at least three or four, if our estimate was correct – but were they part of the war force or rogue madmen? If they were warriors, they should be more careful about how they killed — sane vampaneze don't leave the bodies of their victims where humans can find them. But if they were mad, they shouldn't be capable of hiding so skilfully — after three months of searching, we hadn't found a trace of a single vampaneze in the tunnels beneath the city.

Back at the hotel, we entered via the window. We'd rented two rooms on the upper floor, and used the windows to get in and out at night, since we were too dirty and damp to use the lobby. Besides, the less we moved about on the ground, the better — the city was in uproar, with police and soldiers patrolling the streets, arresting anyone who looked out of place.

While Mr Crepsley and Harkat used the bathrooms, I undressed and waited for a free bath. We could have rented three rooms, so we'd each have a bath, but it was safer for

Harkat not to show himself — Mr Crepsley and me could pass for human, but the monstrous-looking, stitched-together Harkat couldn't.

I nearly fell asleep sitting on the end of the bed. The last three months had been long and arduous. Every night we roamed the roofs and tunnels of the city, searching for vampaneze, avoiding the police, soldiers and frightened humans, many of whom had taken to carrying guns and other weapons. It was taking its toll on all of us, but eleven people had died – that we knew of – and more would follow if we didn't stick to our task.

Standing, I walked around the room, trying to stay awake long enough to get into the bath. Sometimes I didn't, and would wake the following night stinking, sweaty and filthy, feeling like something a cat had coughed up.

I thought about my previous visit to this city. I'd been much younger, still learning what it meant to be a half-vampire. I'd met my first and only girlfriend here — Debbie Hemlock. She'd been dark-skinned, full-lipped and bright-eyed. I would have loved to get to know her better. But duty called, the mad vampaneze was killed, and the currents of life swept us apart.

I'd walked by the house where she'd lived with her parents several times since returning, half-hoping she still lived there. But new tenants had moved in and there was no sign of the Hemlocks. Just as well, really — as a half-vampire I aged at a fifth the human rate, so although nearly thirteen years had passed since I last kissed Debbie, I only looked a few years older. Debbie would be a grown woman now. It would have been confusing if we'd run into one another.

The door connecting the bedrooms opened and Harkat entered, drying himself with a huge hotel towel. "The bath's free," he said, wiping around the top of his bald, grey, scarred head with the towel, careful not to irritate his round green eyes, which had no eyelids to protect them.

"Cheers, ears," I grinned, slipping by him. That was an in-joke — Harkat, like all the Little People, had ears, but they were stitched under the skin at the sides of his head, so it looked as if he hadn't any.

Harkat had drained the bath, put the plug back in and turned on the hot tap, so it was almost full with fresh water when I arrived. I tested the temperature, added a dash of cold, turned off the taps and slid in — heavenly! I raised a hand to brush a lock of hair out of my eyes but my arm wouldn't lift all the way — I was too tired. Relaxing, I decided to just lie there a few minutes. I could wash my hair later. To simply lie in the bath and relax ... for a few minutes ... would be...

Without finishing the thought, I fell soundly asleep, and when I awoke it was night again, and I was blue all over from having spent the day in a bath of cold, grimy water.

CHAPTER TWO

WE RETURNED to the hotel at the end of another long, disappointing night. We'd stayed at the same hotel since coming to the city. We hadn't meant to – the plan had been to switch every couple of weeks – but the search for the vampaneze had left us so exhausted, we hadn't been able to muster the energy to go looking for fresh accommodation. Even the sturdy Harkat Mulds, who didn't need to sleep very much, was dozing off for four or five hours each day.

I felt better after a hot bath and flicked on the TV to see if there was any news about the killings. I learnt it was early Thursday morning – days melted into one another when you lived among vampires, and I rarely took any notice of them – and no new deaths had been reported. It had been almost two weeks since the last body was discovered. There was the slightest hint of hope in the air — many people thought the reign of terror had come to an end. I doubted we'd be that lucky, but I kept my fingers crossed as I turned the set off and headed for the welcome hotel bed.

Sometime later I was roughly shaken awake. A strong light was shining through the thin material of the curtains and I knew instantly that it was midday or early afternoon, which was way too soon to be even thinking about getting out of bed. Grunting, I sat up and found an anxious-looking Harkat leaning over me.

"Wassup?" I muttered, rubbing the grains of sleep from my eyes.

"Someone's knocking at ... your door," Harkat croaked.

"Tell them to please go away," I said — or words to that effect!

"I was going to, but..." He paused.

"Who is it?" I asked, sensing trouble.

"I don't know. I opened the door of *my* room a crack ... and checked. It's nobody connected with the hotel, although ... there's a staff member with him. He's a small man, carrying a big ... briefcase, and he's..." Again Harkat paused. "Come see for yourself."

I got up as there was a round of fresh knuckle raps. I hurried through to Harkat's room. Mr Crepsley was sleeping soundly in one of the twin beds. We tiptoed past him and opened the door ever so slightly. One of the figures in the corridor was familiar – the day manager of the hotel – but I'd never seen the other. He was small, as Harkat had said, and thin, with a huge black briefcase. He was wearing a dark grey suit, black shoes and an old-fashioned bowler hat. He was scowling and raising his knuckles to knock again as we closed the door.

"Think we should answer?" I asked Harkat.

"Yes," he said. "He doesn't look like the sort who'll ... go away if we ignore him."

"Who do you think he is?"

"I'm not sure, but there's something ... officious about him. He might be a police officer or in ... the army."

"You don't think they know about...?" I nodded at the sleeping vampire.

"They'd send more than one man ... if they did," Harkat replied.

I thought about it for a moment, then made up my mind. "I'll go see what he wants. But I won't let him in unless I have to — I don't want people snooping around in here while Mr Crepsley's resting."

"Shall I stay here?" Harkat asked.

"Yes, but keep close to the door and don't lock it — I'll call if I run into trouble."

Leaving Harkat to fetch his axe, I quickly pulled on a pair of trousers and a shirt and went to see what the man in the corridor wanted. Pausing by the door, not opening it, I cleared my throat and called out innocently, "Who is it?"

In immediate response, in a voice like a small dog's bark, the man with the briefcase said, "Mr Horston?"

"No," I replied, breathing a small sigh of relief. "You have the wrong room."

"Oh?" The man in the corridor sounded surprised. "This isn't Mr Vur Horston's room?"

"No, it's—" I winced. I'd forgotten the false names we'd given when registering! Mr Crepsley had signed in as Vur Horston and I'd said I was his son. (Harkat had crept in when no one was watching.) "I mean," I began again, "this is *my* room, not my dad's. I'm Darren Horston, his son."

"Ah." I could sense his smile through the door. "Excellent. You're the reason I'm here. Is your father with you?"

"He's..." I hesitated. "Why do you want to know? Who are you?"

"If you open the door and let me in, I'll explain."

"I'd like to know who you are first," I said. "These are dangerous times. I've been told not to open the door to strangers."

"Ah. Excellent," the little man said again. "I should of course not expect you to open the door to an unannounced visitor. Forgive me. My name is Mr Blaws."

"Blores?"

"*Blaws*," he said, and patiently spelt it out.

"What do you want, Mr Blaws?" I asked.

"I'm a school inspector," he replied. "I've come to find out why you aren't in school."

My jaw dropped about a thousand kilometres.

"May I come in, Darren?" Mr Blaws asked. When I didn't answer, he rapped on the door again and sung out, "Darrrrennn?"

"Um. Just a minute, please," I muttered, then turned my back to the door and leant weakly against it, wildly wondering what I should do.

If I turned the inspector away, he'd return with help, so in the end I opened the door and let him in. The hotel manager departed once he saw that everything was OK, leaving me alone with the serious-looking Mr Blaws. The little man set his briefcase down on the floor, then removed his bowler hat and held it in his left hand, behind his back, as he shook my hand with his right. He was studying me carefully. There was a light layer of bristle on my chin, my hair was long and scruffy, and my face still carried small scars and burn marks from my Trials of Initiation seven years before.

"You look quite old," Mr Blaws commented, sitting down without being asked. "Very mature for fifteen. Maybe it's the hair. You could do with a trim and a shave."

"I guess..." I didn't know why he thought I was fifteen, and I was too bewildered to correct him.

"So!" he boomed, laying his bowler hat aside and his huge briefcase across his lap. "Your father – Mr Horston – is he in?"

"Um ... yeah. He's ... sleeping." I was finding it hard to string words together.

"Oh, of course. I forgot he was on night shifts. Perhaps I should call back at a more convenient..." He trailed off, thumbed open his briefcase, dug out a sheet of paper and studied it as though it was an historical document. "Ah," he said. "Not possible to rearrange — I'm on a tight schedule. You'll have to wake him."

"Um. Right. I'll go ... see if he's..." I hurried through to where the vampire lay sleeping and anxiously shook him awake. Harkat stood back, saying nothing — he'd heard everything and was just as confused as I was.

Mr Crepsley opened one eye, saw that it was daytime, and shut it again. "Is the hotel on fire?" he groaned.

"No."

"Then go away and—"

"There's a man in my room. A school inspector. He knows our names — at least, the names we checked in under — and he thinks I'm fifteen. He wants to know why I'm not at school."

Mr Crepsley shot out of bed as though he'd been bitten. "How can this be?" he snapped. He rushed to the door, stopped, then retreated slowly. "How did he identify himself?"

"Just told me his name — Mr Blaws."

"It could be a cover story."

"I don't think so. The manager of the hotel was with him. He wouldn't have let him up if he wasn't on the level. Besides, he *looks* like a school inspector."

"Looks can be deceptive," Mr Crepsley noted.

"Not this time," I said. "You'd better get dressed and come meet him."

The vampire hesitated, then nodded sharply. I left him to prepare, and went to close the curtains in my room. Mr Blaws looked at me oddly. "My father's eyes are very sensitive," I said. "That's why he prefers to work at night."

"Ah," Mr Blaws said. "Excellent."

We said nothing more for the next few minutes, while we waited for my 'father' to make his entrance. I felt very uncomfortable, sitting in silence with this stranger, but he acted as though he felt perfectly at home. When Mr Crepsley finally entered, Mr Blaws stood and shook his hand, not letting go of the briefcase. "Mr Horston," the inspector beamed. "A pleasure, sir."

"Likewise." Mr Crepsley smiled briefly, then sat as far away from the curtains as he could and drew his red robes tightly around himself.

"So!" Mr Blaws boomed after a short silence. "What's wrong with our young trooper?"

"Wrong?" Mr Crepsley blinked. "Nothing is wrong."

"Then why isn't he at school with all the other boys and girls?"

"Darren does not go to school," Mr Crepsley said, as though speaking to an idiot. "Why should he?"

Mr Blaws was taken aback. "Why, to learn, Mr Horston, the same as any other fifteen year old."

"Darren is not..." Mr Crepsley stopped. "How do you know his age?" he asked cagily.

"From his birth certificate, of course," Mr Blaws laughed.

Mr Crepsley glanced at me for an answer, but I was as lost as he was, and could only shrug helplessly. "And how did you acquire that?" the vampire asked.

Mr Blaws looked at us strangely. "You included it with the rest of the relevant forms when you enrolled him at Mahler's," he said.

"*Mahler's?*" Mr Crepsley repeated.

"The school you chose to send Darren to."

Mr Crepsley sank back in his chair and brooded on that. Then he asked to see the birth certificate, along with the other 'relevant forms'. Mr Blaws reached into his briefcase again and fished out a folder. "There you go," he said. "Birth certificate, records from his previous school, medical certificates, the enrolment form you filled in. Everything present and correct."

Mr Crepsley opened the file, flicked through a few sheets, studied the signatures at the bottom of one form, then passed the file across to me. "Look through those papers," he said. "Check that the information is ... *correct.*"

It wasn't correct, of course – I wasn't fifteen and hadn't been to school recently; nor had I visited a doctor since joining the ranks of the undead – but it was fully detailed. The files built up a complete picture of a fifteen-year-old boy called Darren Horston, who'd moved to this city during the summer with his father, a man who worked night shifts in a local abattoir and...

My breath caught in my throat — the abattoir was the one where we'd first encountered the mad vampaneze, Murlough, thirteen years ago! "Look at this!" I gasped, holding the form out to Mr Crepsley, but he waved it away.

"Is it *accurate?*" he asked.

"Of course it's accurate," Mr Blaws answered. "You filled in the forms yourself." His eyes narrowed. "Didn't you?"

"Of course he did," I said quickly, before Mr Crepsley

could reply. "Sorry to act so befuddled. It's been a hard week. Um. Family problems."

"Ah. That's why you haven't shown up at Mahler's?"

"Yes." I forced a shaky smile. "We should have rung and informed you. Sorry. Didn't think."

"No problem," Mr Blaws said, taking the papers back. "I'm glad that's all it was. We were afraid something bad had happened to you."

"No," I said, shooting Mr Crepsley a look that said, 'play ball'. "Nothing bad happened."

"Excellent. Then you'll be in on Monday?"

"Monday?"

"Hardly seems worth while coming in tomorrow, what with it being the end of the week. Come early Monday morning and we'll sort you out with a timetable and show you around. Ask for—"

"Excuse me," Mr Crepsley interrupted, "but Darren will not be going to your school on Monday or any other day."

"Oh?" Mr Blaws frowned and gently closed the lid of his briefcase. "Has he enrolled at another school?"

"No. Darren does not need to go to school. *I* educate him."

"Really? There was no mention in the forms of your being a qualified teacher."

"I am not a—"

"And of course," Blaws went on, "we both know that only a qualified teacher can educate a child at home." He smiled like a shark. "Don't we?"

Mr Crepsley didn't know what to say. He had no experience of the modern educational system. When he was a boy, parents could do what they liked with their children. I decided to take matters into my own hands.

"Mr Blaws?"

"Yes, Darren?"

"What would happen if I didn't turn up at Mahler's?"

He sniffed snootily. "If you enrol at a different school and pass on the paperwork to me, everything will be fine."

"And if – for the sake of argument – I didn't enrol at another school?"

Mr Blaws laughed. "Everyone has to go to school. Once you turn sixteen, your time is your own, but for the next..." He opened the briefcase again and checked his files "...seven months, you must go to school."

"So if I chose not to go...?"

"We'd send a social worker to see what the problem was."

"And if we asked you to tear up my enrolment form and forget about me – if we said we'd sent it to you by mistake – what then?"

Mr Blaws drummed his fingers on the top of his bowler hat. He wasn't used to such bizarre questions and didn't know what to make of us. "We can't go around tearing up official forms, Darren," he chuckled uneasily.

"But if we'd sent them by accident and wanted to withdraw them?"

He shook his head firmly. "We weren't aware of your existence before you contacted us, but now that we are, we're responsible for you. We'd have to chase you up if we thought you weren't getting a proper education."

"Meaning you'd send social workers after us?"

"Social workers first," he agreed, then looked at us with a glint in his eye. "Of course, if you gave them a hard time, we'd have to call in the police next, and who knows where it would end."

I took that information on board, nodded grimly, then faced Mr Crepsley. "You know what this means, don't you?" He stared back uncertainly. "You'll have to start making packed lunches for me!"

CHAPTER THREE

"MEDDLING, SMUG, stupid little..." Mr Crepsley snarled. He was pacing the hotel room, cursing the name of Mr Blaws. The school inspector had left and Harkat had rejoined us. He'd heard everything through the thin connecting door, but could make no more sense of it than us. "I will track him down tonight and bleed him dry," Mr Crepsley vowed. "That will teach him not to come poking his nose in!"

"Talk like that won't fix this," I sighed. "We have to use our heads."

"Who says it is talk?" Mr Crepsley retorted. "He gave us his telephone number in case we need to contact him. I will find his address and—"

"It's a mobile phone," I sighed. "You can't trace addresses through them. Besides, what good would killing him do? Somebody else would replace him. Our records are on file. He's only the messenger."

"We could move," Harkat suggested. "Find a new hotel."

"No," Mr Crepsley said. "He has seen our faces and would broadcast our descriptions. It would make matters more complicated than they already are."

"What I want to know is *how* our records were submitted," I said. "The signatures on the files weren't ours, but they were pretty damn close."

"I know," he grunted. "Not a great forgery, but adequate."

"Is it possible there's been ... a mix-up?" Harkat asked. "Perhaps a real Vur Horston and his son ... sent in the forms, and you've been confused with them."

"No," I said. "The address of this hotel was included and so were our room numbers. And..." I told them about the abattoir.

Mr Crepsley stopped pacing. "*Murlough!*" he hissed. "That was a period of history I thought I would never have to revisit."

"I don't understand," Harkat said. "How could this be connected to Murlough? Are you saying he's alive and has ... set you up?"

"No," Mr Crepsley said. "Murlough is definitely dead. But someone must know we killed him. And that someone is almost certainly responsible for the humans who have been killed recently." He sat down and rubbed the long scar that marked the left side of his face. "This is a trap."

There was a long, tense silence.

"It can't be," I said in the end. "How could the vampaneze have found out about Murlough?"

"Desmond Tiny," Mr Crepsley said bleakly. "*He* knew about our run in with Murlough, and must have told the vampaneze. But I cannot understand why they faked the birth certificate and school records. If they knew so much about us, and where we are, they should have killed us cleanly and honourably, as is the vampaneze way."

"That's true," I noted. "You don't punish a murderer by sending him to school. Although," I added, remembering my long-ago schooldays, "death *can* sometimes seem preferable to double science on a Thursday afternoon..."

Again a lengthy silence descended. Harkat broke it by clearing his throat. "This sounds crazy," the Little Person said, "but what if Mr Crepsley *did* ... submit the forms?"

"Come again?" I said.

"He might have done it in ... his sleep."

"You think he *sleep wrote* a birth cert and school records, then submitted them to a local school?" I didn't even bother to laugh.

"Things like this have happened before," Harkat mumbled. "Remember Pasta O'Malley at the ... Cirque Du Freak? He read books at night when he was asleep. He could never recall reading them, but if you asked ... him about them, he could answer all your questions."

"I'd forgotten about Pasta," I muttered, giving Harkat's proposal some thought.

"I could not have filled in those forms," Mr Crepsley said stiffly.

"It's unlikely," Harkat agreed, "but we do strange things ... when we sleep. Perhaps you—"

"No," Mr Crepsley interrupted. "You do not understand. I could not have done it because..." He looked away sheepishly. "I cannot read or write."

The vampire might have had two heads, the way Harkat and me gawped at him.

"Of course you can read and write!" I bellowed. "You signed your name when we checked in."

"Signing one's name is an easy feat," he replied quietly, with wounded dignity. "I can read numbers and recognize certain words – I am able to read maps quite accurately – but as for genuine reading and writing..." He shook his head.

"How can you not be able to read or write?" I asked ignorantly.

"Things were different when I was young. The world was simpler. It was not necessary to be a master of the written word. I was the fifth child of a poor family and went to work at the age of eight."

"But ... but..." I pointed a finger at him. "You told me you love Shakespeare's plays and poems!"

"I do," he said. "Evanna read all his works to me over the decades. Wordsworth, Keats, Joyce — many others. I often meant to learn to read for myself, but I never got around to it."

"This is ... I don't... Why didn't you tell me?" I snapped. "We've been together fifteen years, and this is the first time you've mentioned it!"

He shrugged. "I assumed you knew. Many vampires are illiterate. That is why so little of our history or laws is written down — most of us are incapable of reading."

Shaking my head, exasperated, I put aside the vampire's revelation and concentrated on the more immediate problem. "You didn't fill out the forms — that's settled. So who did and what are we going to do about it?"

Mr Crepsley had no answer to that, but Harkat had a suggestion. "It could have been Mr Tiny," he said. "He loves to stir things up. Perhaps this is his idea ... of a joke."

We mulled that one over.

"It has a whiff of him about it," I agreed. "I can't see why he'd want to send me back to school, but it's the sort of trick I can imagine him pulling."

"Mr Tiny would appear to be the most logical culprit," Mr Crepsley said. "Vampaneze are not known for their sense of humour. Nor do they go in for intricate plots — like vampires, they are simple and direct."

"Let's say he *is* behind it," I mused. "That still leaves us with the problem of what to do. Should I report for class Monday morning? Or do we ignore Mr Blaws' warning and carry on as before?"

"I would rather not send you," Mr Crepsley said. "There is strength in unity. At present, we are well prepared to defend ourselves should we come under attack. With you at school, we would not be there to help you if you ran into trouble, and you would not be able to help us if our foes struck here."

"But if I don't go," I noted, "we'll have school inspectors — and worse — dogging our heels."

"The other option is to leave," Harkat said. "Just pack our bags and go."

"That is worth considering," Mr Crepsley agreed. "I do not like the idea of leaving these people to suffer, but if this *is* a trap designed to divide us, perhaps the killings will stop if we leave."

"Or they might increase," I said, "to tempt us back."

We thought about it some more, weighing up the various options.

"I want to stay," Harkat said eventually. "Life is getting more dangerous, but perhaps ... that means we're meant to be here. Maybe this city is where we're destined ... to lock horns with the Vampaneze Lord again."

"I agree with Harkat," Mr Crepsley said, "but this is a matter for Darren to decide. As a Prince, he must make the decision."

"Thanks a lot," I said sarcastically.

Mr Crepsley smiled. "It is your decision, not only because you are a Prince, but because this concerns you the most — *you* will have to mix with human children and teachers, and *you* will be the most vulnerable to attack. Whether this is a vampaneze trap or a whim of Mr Tiny's, life will be hard for you if we stay."

He was right. Going back to school would be a nightmare. I'd no idea what fifteen year olds studied. Classes would be hard. Homework would drive me loopy. And having to answer to teachers, after six years of lording it over the vampires as a Prince... It could get very uncomfortable.

Yet part of me was drawn to the notion. To sit in a classroom again, to learn, make friends, show off my advanced physical skills in PE, maybe go out with a few girls...

"The hell with it," I grinned. "If it's a trap, let's call their bluff. If it's a joke, we'll show we know how to take it."

"That is the spirit," Mr Crepsley boomed.

"Besides," I chuckled weakly, "I've endured the Trials of Initiation twice, a terrifying journey through an underground stream, encounters with killers, a bear and wild boars. How bad can *school* be?"

CHAPTER FOUR

I ARRIVED at Mahler's an hour before classes began. I'd had a busy weekend. First there'd been my uniform to buy – a green jumper, light green shirt, green tie, grey trousers, black shoes – then books, notepaper and A4 writing pads, a ruler, pens and pencils, an eraser, set squares and a compass, as well as a scientific calculator, whose array of strange buttons – 'INV', 'SIN', 'COS', 'EE' – meant nothing to me. I'd also had to buy a homework report book, which I'd have to write all my homework assignments in — Mr Crepsley would have to sign the book each night, saying I'd done the work I was meant to.

I shopped by myself — Mr Crepsley couldn't move about during the day, and Harkat's strange appearance meant it was better for him to stay inside. I got back to the hotel with my bags late Saturday evening, after two days of non-stop shopping. Then I remembered that I'd need a schoolbag as well, so I rushed out on one last-gasp, lightning-fast expedition to the nearest supplier. I bought a simple black bag with plenty of space for my books, and picked up a plastic lunch box as well.

Mr Crepsley and Harkat got a great kick out of my uniform. The first time they saw me stuffed inside it, walking stiffly, they laughed for ten minutes. "Stop it!" I growled, tearing a shoe off and lobbing it at them.

I spent Sunday wearing in the uniform, walking about the hotel rooms fully dressed. I did a lot of scratching and twitching — it had been a long time since I'd had to wear anything so confining. That night I shaved carefully and let Mr Crepsley cut my hair. Afterwards he and Harkat left to hunt for the vampaneze. For the first night since coming to the city, I stayed behind — I had school in the morning, and needed to be fresh for it. As time progressed, I'd work out a schedule whereby I'd assist in the hunt for the killers, but the first few nights were bound to be difficult and we all agreed it would be for the best if I dropped out of the hunt for a while.

I got hardly any sleep. I was almost as nervous as I'd been seven years earlier, when awaiting the verdict of the Vampire Princes after I'd failed my Trials of Initiation. At least then I knew what the worst could be – death – but I'd no idea what to expect from this strange adventure.

Mr Crepsley and Harkat were awake in the morning to see me off. They ate breakfast with me and tried to act as though I'd nothing to worry about. "This is a wonderful opportunity," Mr Crepsley said. "You have often complained of the life you lost when you became a half-vampire. This is a chance to revisit your past. You can be human again, for a while. It will be fascinating."

"Why don't you go instead of me then?" I snapped.

"I would if I could," he deadpanned.

"It'll be fun," Harkat assured me. "Strange at first, but give it time and you'll fit in. And don't feel inferior: these kids will know ... a lot more about the school curriculum than you, but you are ... a man of the world and know things that they will ... never learn, no matter how old they live to be."

"You are a Prince," Mr Crepsley agreed, "far superior to any there."

Their efforts didn't really help, but I was glad they were supporting me instead of mocking me.

With breakfast out of the way, I made a few ham sandwiches, packed them in my bag along with a small jar of pickled onions and a bottle of orange juice, and then it was time to leave.

"Do you want me to walk you to school?" Mr Crepsley asked innocently. "There are many dangerous roads to cross. Or perhaps you could ask a lollypop lady to hold your hand and—"

"Stuff it," I grunted, and bolted out the door with my bag full of books.

Mahler's was a large, modern school, the buildings arranged in a square around an open-air, cement recreational area. The main doors were open when I arrived, so I entered and went looking for the headmaster's room. The halls and rooms were clearly signposted, and I found Mr Chivers' room within a couple of minutes, but there was no sign of the headmaster. Half an hour passed — no Mr Chivers. I wondered if Mr Blaws had forgotten to tell the headmaster of my early arrival, but then I recalled the little man with the huge briefcase, and knew he wasn't the sort who forgot things like that. Maybe Mr Chivers thought he was supposed to meet me by the main doors or the staffroom. I decided to check.

The staffroom could have held twenty-five or thirty teachers, but I saw only three when I knocked and entered in response to a cry of, "Come in." Two were middle-aged men, glued to thick chairs, reading enormous newspapers. The other was a burly woman, busy pinning sheets of printed paper to the walls.

"Help you?" the woman snapped without looking around.

"My name's Darren Horston. I'm looking for Mr Chivers."

"Mr Chivers isn't in yet. Have you an appointment?"

"Um. Yes. I think so."

"Then wait for him outside his office. This is the *staffroom*."

"Oh. OK."

Closing the door, I picked up my bag and returned to the headmaster's room. There was still no sign of him. I waited ten more minutes, then went searching for him again. This time I made for the school entrance, where I found a group of teenagers leaning against a wall, talking loudly, yawning, laughing, calling each other names and cursing pleasantly.

They were dressed in Mahler uniforms like me, but the clothes looked natural on them.

I approached a gang of five boys and two girls. They had their backs to me and were discussing some programme they'd seen on TV the night before. I cleared my throat to attract their attention, then smiled and stuck out a hand to the nearest boy when he turned. "Darren Horston," I grinned. "I'm new here. I'm looking for Mr Chivers. You haven't seen him, have you?"

The boy stared at my hand – he didn't shake it – then into my face.

"You wot?" he mumbled.

"My name's Darren Horston," I said again. "I'm looking for–"

"I 'eard you the first time," he interrupted, scratching his nose and studying me suspiciously.

"Shivers ain't in yet," a girl said, and giggled as though she'd said something funny.

"Shivers ain't ever in before ten past nine," one of the boys yawned.

"An' even later on a Monday," the girl said.

"*Everyone* knows *that*," the boy who'd first spoken added.

"Oh," I muttered. "Well, as I said, I'm new here, so I can't be expected to know things that everyone else knows, can I?" I smiled, pleased to have made such a clever point on my first day in school.

"Get stuffed, asswipe," the boy said in response, which wasn't exactly what I'd been expecting.

"Pardon?" I blinked.

"You 'eard." He squared up to me. He was about a head taller, dark-haired, with a nasty squint. I could knock the stuffing out of any human in the school, but I'd momentarily forgotten that, and backed away from him, unsure of why he was acting this way.

"Go on, Smickey," one of the other boys laughed. "Do 'im!"

"Nah," the boy called Smickey smirked. "He ain't worth it."

Turning his back on me, he resumed his conversation with the others as though nothing had interrupted it. Shaken and confused, I slouched away. As I turned the corner, out of human but not vampire hearing, I heard one of the girls say, "That guy's seriously weird!"

"See that bag he was carrying?" Smickey laughed. "It was the size of a cow! He must have half the books in the country in it!"

"He spoke weird," the girl said.

"And he looked even weirder," the other girl added. "Those scars and red patches of flesh. And did you see that awful haircut? He looked like somefing out of a zoo!"

"Too right," Smickey said. "He smelt like it too!"

The gang laughed, then talk turned to the TV programme again. Trudging up the stairs, clutching my bag to my chest, feeling very small and ashamed of my hair and appearance, I positioned myself by Mr Chivers' door, hung my head, and miserably waited for the headmaster to show.

It had been a discouraging start, and though I liked to think things could only get better, I had a nasty feeling in the pit of my belly that they were going to get a whole lot worse!

CHAPTER FIVE

MR CHIVERS arrived shortly after a quarter past nine, puffing and red-faced. (I later learnt that he cycled to school.) He hurried past me without saying anything, opened the door to his room, and stumbled to the window, where he stood staring down at the cement quad. Spotting someone, he slid open the window and roared, "Kevin O'Brien! Have you been kicked out of class already?"

"Wasn't my fault, sir," a young boy shouted back. "The top came off my pen in my bag, ruining my homework. Could have happened to anyone, sir. I don't think I should be kicked out for—"

"Report to my office during your next free period, O'Brien!" Mr Chivers interrupted. "I have a few floors for you to scrub."

"Aw, sir!"

Mr Chivers slammed the window shut. "You!" he said, beckoning me in. "What are you here for?"

"I'm—"

"You didn't break a window, did you?" he cut in. "Because if you did, there'll be hell and leather to pay!"

"I didn't break a window," I snapped. "I haven't had time to break anything. I've been stuck outside your door since eight, waiting. You're late!"

"Oh?" He sat down, surprised by my directness. "Sorry. A flat tyre. It's the little monster who lives two floors below. He…" Clearing his throat, he remembered who he was and adopted a scowl. "Never mind about me — who are you and why were you waiting?"

"My name's Darren Horston. I'm—"

"—the new boy!" he exclaimed. "Sorry — clean forgot you were coming." Getting up, he took my hand and pumped it. "I was away this weekend – orienteering – only got back last night. I jotted down a note and pinned it to the fridge on Friday, but I must have missed it this morning."

"No problem," I said, freeing my fingers from his sweaty hand. "You're here now. Better late than never."

He studied me curiously. "Is that how you addressed your previous headmaster?" he asked.

I remembered how I used to tremble when faced with the headmistress of my old school. "No," I chuckled.

"Good, because it's not how you'll address me either. I'm no tyrant, but I don't stand for backchat. Speak respectfully when you talk to me, and add a 'sir' at the end. Got that?"

I took a deep breath. "Yes." A pause. "Sir."

"Better," he grunted, then invited me to sit. Opening a drawer, he found a file and perused it in silence. "Good grades," he said after a couple of minutes, laying it aside. "If you can match those here, we won't complain."

"I'll do my best. Sir."

"That's all we ask." Mr Chivers was studying my face, fascinated by my scars and burn-marks. "You've had a rough ride, haven't you?" he remarked. "Must be horrible to be trapped in a burning building."

"Yes, sir." That was in the report Mr Blaws had shown me — according to the forms my 'father' submitted, I'd been badly burnt in a house fire when I was twelve.

"Still, all's well that ends well! You're alive and active, and anything else is a bonus." Standing, he put the file away, checked the front of his suit – there were traces of egg and toast crumbs on his tie and shirt, which he picked at – then made for the door, telling me to follow.

Mr Chivers led me on a quick tour of the school, pointing out the computer rooms, assembly hall, gymnasium and the main classrooms. The school used to be a music academy, hence its name (Mahler was a famous composer), but had closed down twenty years earlier, before reopening as a regular school.

"We still place a lot of emphasis on musical excellence," Mr Chivers told me as we checked out a large room with half a dozen pianos. "Do you play any instruments?"

"The flute," I said.

"A flautist! Superb! We haven't had a decent flautist since

47

Siobhan Toner graduated three — or was it four? — years ago. We'll have to try you out, see what you're made of, eh?"

"Yes, sir," I replied weakly. I figured we were talking at cross purposes — he was referring to real flutes, whereas all I knew how to play was a tin-whistle — but I didn't know whether it was the time for me to point this out. In the end I kept my mouth shut and hoped he'd forget about my supposed flute-playing talents.

He told me each lesson lasted forty minutes. There was a ten-minute break at eleven o'clock; fifty minutes for lunch at ten past one; school finished at four. "Detention runs from four-thirty to six," he informed me, "but hopefully that won't concern you, eh?"

"I hope not, sir," I replied meekly.

The tour concluded back at his office, where he furnished me with my timetable. It was a frightening list — English, history, geography, science, maths, mechanical drawing, two modern languages, computer studies. A double dose of PE on Wednesdays. I had three free periods, one on Monday, one on Tuesday, one on Thursday. Mr Chivers said these were for extra-curricular activities, such as music or extra languages, or they could be used as study classes.

He shook my hand again, wished me the best of luck and told me to call on him if I ran into difficulty. After warning me not to break any windows or give my teachers grief he showed me out into the corridor, where he left me. It was 9.40 A bell rang. Time for my first class of the day — geography.

The lesson went reasonably well. I'd spent the last six years poring over maps and keeping abreast of the War of the Scars, so I had a better idea of the shape of the world than most of my classmates. But I knew nothing about *human* geography – a lot of the lesson revolved around economies and culture, and how humans shaped their environments – and I was at a loss every time talk switched from mountain ranges and rivers to political systems and population statistics.

Even allowing for my limited knowledge of humans, geography was as easy a start as I could have wished for. The teacher was helpful, I was able to keep up with most of what was being discussed, and I thought I'd be able to catch up with the rest of the class within a few weeks.

Maths, which came next, was a different matter entirely. I knew after five minutes that I was in trouble. I'd covered only basic maths in school, and had forgotten most of the little I used to know. I could divide and multiply, but that was as far as my expertise stretched — which, I quickly discovered, wasn't nearly far enough.

"What do you mean, you've never done algebra?" my teacher, a fierce man by the name of Mr Smarts, snapped. "Of course you have! Don't take me for a fool, lad. I know you're new, but don't think that means you can get away with murder. Open that book to page sixteen and do the first set of problems. I'll collect your work at the end of class and see where you stand."

Where I stood was outside in the cold, a hundred kilometres distant. I couldn't even *read* the problems on page sixteen, never mind solve them! I looked through the earlier pages and tried copying the examples set there, but I hadn't a clue what I was doing. When Mr Smarts took my copy from me and said he'd check it during lunch and return it to me that afternoon in science – I had him for that as well – I was too downhearted to thank him for his promptness.

Break was no better. I spent the ten minutes wandering alone, being stared at by everyone in the yard. I tried making friends with some of the people I recognized from my first two classes, but they wanted nothing to do with me. I looked, smelt and acted weird, and there was something *not right* about me. The teachers hadn't sussed me out yet, but the kids had. They knew I didn't belong.

Even if my fellow students had tried making me feel welcome, I'd have struggled to adapt. I knew nothing of the films and TV shows they were discussing, or the rock stars or styles of music, or the books and comics. Their way of speaking was strange too — I couldn't understand a lot of their slang.

I had history after the break. That used to be one of my favourite subjects, but this syllabus was far more advanced than mine had been. The class was focusing on World War II, which was what I'd been studying during my last few months as a human. Back then I'd only had to learn the major events of the war, and the leaders of the various countries. But as a fifteen year old, who'd supposedly progressed through the system, I was expected to know the detailed ins and outs of battles, the names of generals, the wide-ranging social effects of the war, and so on.

I told my teacher I'd been concentrating on ancient history in my old school, and complimented myself on such a clever answer — but then she said there was a small class of ancient history students at Mahler's and she'd get me transferred first thing tomorrow.

Ai-yi-yi-yi-yi!

English next. I was dreading it. I could bluff my way through subjects like geography and history, by saying I'd been following a different syllabus. But how was I going to explain my shortcomings in English? I could pretend not to have read all the books and poems that the others had, but what would happen when my teacher asked what I'd read instead? I was doomed!

There was a free table close to the front of the class, where I had to sit. Our teacher was late — because of the size of the school, teachers and pupils often arrived slightly late for class. I spent a couple of minutes anxiously scanning the book of poetry I'd bought last Friday, desperately committing a few scraps of random poems to memory, in the hope that I could fob the teacher off with them.

The door to the classroom opened, the noise level dropped, and everyone stood up. "Sit down, sit down," the teacher said, making straight for her desk, where she laid her stack of books. Facing the class, she smiled and brushed her hair back. She was a young, pretty black woman. "I hear we've a new addition," she said, looking around the room for me. "Will you stand up please, so I can identify you?"

Standing, I raised a hand and smiled edgily. "Here," I said.

"Close to the front," she beamed. "A good sign. Now, I have your name and details written down somewhere. Just give me a minute and I'll..."

She was turning aside to look among her books and papers, when all of a sudden she stopped as though slapped, glanced sharply at me and took a step forward. Her face lit up and she exclaimed, "*Darren Shan?*"

"Um. Yes." I smiled nervously. I'd no idea who she was, and was scouring my memory banks – was she staying in the same hotel as me? – when something about the shape of her mouth and eyes jogged a switch inside my brain. Leaving my table, I took several steps towards her, until we were only a metre apart, then studied her face incredulously. "*Debbie?*" I gasped. "*Debbie Hemlock?*"

CHAPTER SIX

"DARREN!" DEBBIE squealed, throwing her arms around me.

"Debbie!" I whooped and hugged her hard.

My English teacher was Debbie Hemlock — my ex-girlfriend!

"You've barely changed!" Debbie gasped.

"You look so different!" I laughed.

"What happened to your face?"

"How did you become a teacher?"

Then, together: "What are you doing here?"

We stopped, wide-eyed, beaming madly. We were no longer hugging, but our hands were joined. Around us, my fellow students gawped as though they were witnessing the end of the universe.

"Where have..." Debbie started, then glanced around. Realizing we were the centre of attention, she let go of my hands and smiled sheepishly. "Darren and I are old friends," she explained to the class. "We haven't seen each other in..."

Again she stopped, this time with a frown. "Excuse us," she muttered, grabbing my right hand and roughly leading the way outside. Closing the door, she swung me up against a wall, checked to make sure we were alone in the hall, leant in close and hissed, "Where the hell have you been all these years?"

"Here and there," I smiled, eyes roving her face, stunned by how much she'd changed. She was taller too — even taller than me now.

"Why is your face the same?" she snapped. "You look almost exactly as I remember you. You've aged a year or two, but it's been *thirteen* years!"

"How time flies," I smirked, then stole a quick kiss. "Good to see you again, Miss Hemlock."

Debbie froze at the kiss, then took a step back. "Don't do that."

"Sorry. Just glad to see you."

"I'm glad to see you too. But if anyone sees me kissing a student..."

"Oh, Debbie, I'm not really a student. You know that. I'm old enough to be... Well, you know how old I am."

"I thought I did. But your face..." She traced the outline of my jaw, then my lips and nose, then the small triangular scar above my right eye. "You've been in the wars," she noted.

"You wouldn't believe it if I told you how right you are," I smiled.

"Darren Shan." She shook her head and repeated my name. "Darren Shan."

Then she slapped me!

"What's that for?" I yelped.

"For leaving without saying goodbye and ruining my Christmas," she growled.

"That was thirteen years ago. Surely you're not still upset about it."

"The Hemlocks can carry a grudge a long, long time," she said, but there was the glint of a smile in her eyes.

"I did leave you a going-away present," I said.

For a moment her face was blank. Then she remembered. "The tree!"

Mr Crepsley and me had killed the mad vampaneze – Murlough – in Debbie's house on Christmas Eve, after using her as bait to lure him out of his lair. Before leaving, I'd placed a small Christmas tree by her bedside and decorated it (I'd drugged Debbie and her parents earlier, so they were unconscious when Murlough attacked).

"I'd forgotten about the tree," she muttered. "Which brings us to another point — what happened back then? One moment we were sitting down to dinner, the next I woke up in bed and it was late Christmas Day. Mum and Dad woke in their beds too, with no idea of how they got there."

"How are Donna and Jesse?" I asked, trying to avoid her question.

"Fine. Dad's still travelling the world, going wherever his work takes him, and Mum's started a new... No," she said, prodding me in the chest. "Forget what's been going on with *me.* I want to know what's up with *you*. For thirteen years you've been a fond memory. I tried finding you a few times, but you'd vanished without a trace. Now you waltz back into my life, looking as though the years had been months. I want to know what gives."

"It's a long story," I sighed. "And complicated."

"I've got time," she sniffed.

"No, you haven't," I contradicted her, nodding at the closed classroom door.

"Damn. I forgot about them." She strode to the door and opened it. The kids inside had been talking loudly, but they stopped at the sight of their teacher. "Get out your books!" she snapped. "I'll be with you presently." Facing me again, she said, "You're right — we don't have time. And my schedule's full for the rest of the day — I've a teachers' meeting to attend during lunch. But we have to get together soon and talk."

"How about after school?" I suggested. "I'll go home, change clothes, and we can meet ... where?"

"My place," Debbie said. "I live on the third floor of an apartment block. 3c, Bungrove Drive. It's about a ten-minute walk from here."

"I'll find it."

"But give me a couple of hours to correct homework," she said. "Don't come before half-six."

"Sounds perfect."

"Darren Shan," she whispered, a small smile lifting the corners of her mouth. "Who'd have believed it?" She leant towards me, and I thought – hoped! – she was going to kiss me, but then she stopped, adopted a stern expression and pushed me back into class ahead of her.

The lesson passed in a blur. Debbie tried hard not to pay special attention to me, but our eyes kept meeting and we were unable to stop smiling. The others kids noted the remarkable bond between us and it was the talk of the school by lunchtime. If the students had been suspicious of me at the start of the day, now they were downright wary, and everyone gave me a wide berth.

I breezed through the later classes. It didn't bother me that I was out of my depth and ignorant of the subject matter. I no longer cared or tried to act clued up. Debbie was all I could think about. Even when Mr Smarts threw my maths copy at me in science and bawled furiously, I only smiled, nodded and tuned him out.

At the end of the day I rushed back to the hotel. I'd been given the key to a locker, where I was supposed to leave my books, but I was so excited I didn't bother with it, and carried the full bag of books home with me. Mr Crepsley was still in bed when I arrived, but Harkat was awake, and I hurriedly told him about my day and meeting Debbie.

"Isn't it wonderful?" I finished breathlessly. "Isn't it incredible? Isn't it the most..." I couldn't think of any way to describe it, so I simply threw my hands into the air and yelled, "Yahoo!"

"It's great," Harkat said, wide mouth spreading into a jagged smile, but he didn't sound happy.

"What's wrong?" I asked, reading the unease in his round green eyes.

"Nothing," he said. "It's great. Really. I'm thrilled for you."

"Don't lie to me, Harkat. Something's bugging you. What?"

He came out with it. "Doesn't this seem a bit ... *too* coincidental?"

"What do you mean?"

"Of all the schools you could have gone to ... all the teachers in the world ... you end up at the one where your ... old girlfriend's teaching? And in her class?"

"Life's like that, Harkat. Strange things happen all the time."

"Yes," the Little Person agreed. "And sometimes they happen ... by chance. But other times they're ... arranged."

I'd been unbuttoning my shirt, having slipped off my jumper and tie. Now I paused, fingers on the buttons, and studied him. "What are you saying?"

"Something smells rotten. If you'd run into Debbie in the street, that ... would be something else. But you're in her class at a school where ... you shouldn't be. Somebody set you up to go to Mahler's, someone who ... knows about Murlough, and about your past."

"You think the person who forged our signatures knew Debbie was working at Mahler's?" I asked.

"That's obvious," Harkat said. "And that in itself is cause for worry. But there's something else we ... must consider. What if the person who set you up didn't ... just *know* about Debbie — what if it *was* Debbie?"

CHAPTER SEVEN

I COULDN'T believe Debbie was in league with the vampaneze or Mr Tiny, or had played any part in setting me up to go to Mahler's. I told Harkat how stunned she'd been to see me, but he said she might have been acting. "If she went to all the trouble of getting ... you there, she'd hardly *not* act surprised," he noted.

I shook my head stubbornly. "She wouldn't do something like this."

"I don't know her, so I can't voice ... an opinion. But *you* don't really know her either. She was a child when you ... last saw her. People change as they grow."

"You don't think I should trust her?"

"I'm not saying that. Maybe she's genuine. Maybe she had nothing to do with faking the ... forms, or with you being there — it *could* be a ... huge coincidence. But caution is required. Go see her, but keep an eye ... on her. Be careful what you say. Put some probing questions to her. And take a weapon."

"I couldn't hurt her," I said quietly. "Even if she has plotted against us, there's no way I could kill her."

"Take one anyway," Harkat insisted. "If she's working with the vampaneze, it may not be ... *her* you have to use it on."

"You reckon the vampaneze could be lying in wait there?"

"Maybe. We couldn't understand why ... the vampaneze — if they're behind the fake forms — would send you ... to school. If they're working with Debbie — or using ... her — this might explain it."

"You mean they want to get me at Debbie's alone, so they can pick me off?"

"They might."

I nodded thoughtfully. I didn't believe Debbie was working with our foes, but it was possible that they were manipulating her to get to me. "How should we handle this?" I asked.

Harkat's green eyes betrayed his uncertainty. "I'm not sure. It would be foolish to walk into ... a trap. But sometimes risks must be taken. Perhaps this is our way to flush out ... those who would ensnare us."

Chewing my lower lip, I brooded upon it a while, then followed the most sensible course of action — I went and woke Mr Crepsley.

I rang the bell for 3c and waited. A moment later, Debbie's voice came over the intercom. "Darren?"

"The one and only."

"You're late." It was twenty past seven. The sun was setting.

"Got stuck doing homework. Blame my English teacher — she's a real dragon."

"Ha-flaming-ha."

There was a buzzing noise and the door opened. I paused before entering and looked across the street at the opposite block of apartments. I spotted a lurking shadow on the roof — Mr Crepsley. Harkat was behind Debbie's building. Both would rush to my rescue at the first sign of trouble. That was the plan we'd hatched. Mr Crepsley had suggested beating a hasty retreat — things were getting too complicated for his liking — but when I pulled rank, he'd agreed to make the most of the situation and attempt to turn the tables on our opponents — *if* they showed.

"If a fight develops," he warned me before setting out, "it may not be possible to choose targets. You are not prepared to raise a hand against your friend, but *I* am, if she is working with the enemy. Do not get in my way if that happens."

I nodded grimly. I wasn't sure I could stand by and let him harm Debbie, even if it turned out that she was conspiring against us — but I'd try.

Trotting up the stairs, I was painfully aware of the two knives I was carrying, strapped to my calves so as not to show. I hoped I wouldn't have to use them, but it was good to know they were there if needed.

The door to 3c was open, but I knocked before entering. "Come in," Debbie called. "I'm in the kitchen."

I closed the door but didn't lock it. Quickly scanned the apartment. Very tidy. Several bookcases, overflowing with books. A CD player and stand; lots of CDs. A portable TV set. A cover poster of *The Lord of the Rings* on one wall, a picture of Debbie with her parents on another.

Debbie stepped in from the kitchen. She was wearing a long red apron and there was flour in her hair. "I got bored waiting for you," she said, "so I started to make scones. Do you like yours with currants or without?"

"Without," I said and smiled as she ducked back into the kitchen — killers and their cohorts don't greet you with flour in their hair! Any half-doubts I had about Debbie quickly vanished and I knew I'd nothing to fear from her. But I didn't drop my guard — Debbie didn't pose a threat, but there might be vampaneze in the room next door or hovering on the fire escape.

"How did you enjoy your first day at school?" Debbie asked, as I wandered round the living room.

"It was strange. I haven't been inside a school since... Well, it's been a long time. So much has changed. When I was..." I stopped. The cover of a book had caught my eye: *The Three Musketeers*. "Is Donna still making you read this?"

Debbie poked her head through the doorway and looked at the book. "Oh," she laughed. "I was reading that when we first met, wasn't I?"

"Yep. You hated it."

"Really? That's odd — I love it now. It's one of my favourites. I recommend it to my pupils all the time."

Shaking my head wryly, I laid the book down and went to view the kitchen. It was small, but professionally organized. There was a lovely smell of fresh dough. "Donna taught you well," I remarked. Debbie's mum used to be a chef.

"She wouldn't let me leave home until I could run a good kitchen," Debbie smiled. "Graduating university was easier than passing the tests she set."

"You've been to university?" I asked.

"I'd hardly be teaching if I hadn't."

Laying a tray of unbaked scones into a petite oven, she switched off the light and motioned me back to the living room. As I flopped into one of the soft chairs she went to the CD stand and looked for something to play. "Any preferences?"

"Not really."

"I don't have much in the way of pop or rock. Jazz or classical?"

"I don't mind."

Choosing a CD, she took it out of its case, inserted it in the player and turned it on. She stood by the player a couple of minutes while flowing, lifting music filled the air. "Like it?" she asked.

"Not bad. What is it?"

"*The Titan.* Do you know who it's by?"

"Mahler?" I guessed.

"Right. I thought I'd play it for you, so you're familiar with it — Mr Chivers gets very upset if his students don't recognize Mahler." Taking the chair next to mine, Debbie studied my face in silence. I felt uncomfortable, but didn't turn away. "So," she sighed. "Want to tell me about it?"

I'd discussed what I should tell her with Mr Crepsley and Harkat, and quickly launched into the story we'd settled upon. I said I was the victim of an ageing disease, which meant I aged slower than normal people. I reminded her of the snake-boy, Evra Von, whom she'd met, and said the two of us were patients at a special clinic.

"You aren't brothers?" she asked.

"No. And the man we were with wasn't our father — he was a nurse at the hospital. That's why I never let you meet him — it was fun, having you think I was an ordinary person, and I didn't want him giving the game away."

"So how old *are* you?" she enquired.

"Not much older than you," I said. "The disease didn't set in until I was twelve. I wasn't very different to other children until then."

She considered that in her careful, thoughtful manner. "If that's true," she said, "what are you doing in school now? And why pick mine?"

"I didn't know you were working at Mahler's," I said. "That's a freak occurrence. I've returned to school because... It's hard to explain. I didn't get a proper education when I was growing up. I was rebellious and spent a lot of time off fishing or playing football when I should have been learning.

Lately I've been feeling like I missed out. A few weeks ago I met a man who forges papers — passports, birth certificates, stuff like that. I asked him to set me up with a fake ID, so I could pretend I was fifteen."

"Whatever for?" Debbie asked. "Why didn't you go to an adult night school?"

"Because, looks-wise, I'm *not* an adult." I pulled a sad face. "You don't know how miserable it gets, growing so slowly, explaining myself to strangers, knowing they're talking about me. I don't mingle much. I live alone and stay indoors most of the time. I felt this was an opportunity to pretend I was normal. I thought I could fit in with the people I most resemble — fifteen year olds. I hoped, if I dressed and talked like them, and went to school with them, maybe they'd accept me and I wouldn't feel so lonely." Lowering my gaze, I added mournfully, "I guess the pretence stops now."

There was a silent beat. Another. Then Debbie said, "Why should it?"

"Because you know about me. You'll tell Mr Chivers. I'll have to leave."

Debbie reached across and took my left hand in hers. "I think you're crazy," she said. "Practically everyone I know couldn't wait to leave school, and here you are, desperate to return. But I admire you for this. I think it's great that you want to learn. I think you're very brave, and I won't say anything about it."

"Really?"

"I think you'll be found out eventually — an act like this is impossible to sustain — but I won't blow the whistle on you."

"Thanks, Debbie. I..." Clearing my throat, I looked at our joined hands. "I'd like to kiss you — to thank you — but I don't know if you want me to."

Debbie frowned, and I could see what she was thinking — was it acceptable for a teacher to let one of her pupils kiss her? Then she chuckled and said, "OK — but just on my cheek."

Lifting my head, I leant over and brushed her cheek with my lips. I would have liked to kiss her properly, but knew I couldn't. Although we were of similar ages, in her eyes I was still a teenager. There was a line between us we couldn't step over — much as the adult within me hungered to cross it.

We talked for hours. I learnt all about Debbie's life, how she'd gone to university after school, studied English and sociology, graduated and went on to become a teacher. After a few part-time appointments elsewhere, she'd applied for a number of permanent positions here — she'd seen out her schooldays in this city, and felt it was the nearest place she had to a home. She ended up at Mahler's. She'd been there two years and loved it. There'd been men in her life — she'd been engaged at one stage! — but none at the moment. And she said — very pointedly — that she wasn't looking for any either!

She asked me about that night thirteen years ago and what had happened to her and her parents. I lied and said there'd been something wrong with the wine. "You all fell asleep at the table. I rang for the nurse who was looking after Evra and me. He came, checked, said you were OK and would be fine when you woke. We put the three of you to bed and I slipped away. I've never been good at saying farewell."

I told Debbie I was living alone. If she checked with Mr Blaws, she'd know that was a lie, but I didn't think ordinary teachers mixed much with inspectors.

"It's going to be bizarre having you in my class," she murmured. We were sitting on the couch. "We'll have to be careful. If anyone suspects there was ever anything between us, we must tell the truth. It'd mean my career if we didn't."

"Maybe it's a problem we won't have to worry about much longer," I said.

"What do you mean?"

"I don't think I'm cut out for school. I'm behind in all the subjects. In some – maths and science – I'm not even within sighting distance of everyone else. I think I'll have to drop out."

"That's quitting talk," she growled, "and I won't stand for it." She popped one of the scones – they were chestnut brown, smeared with butter and jam – into my mouth and made me munch on it. "Finish what you start or you'll regret it."

"Buh I cahn't duh iht," I mumbled, mouth full of scone.

"Of course you can," she insisted. "It won't be easy. You'll have to study hard, maybe get some private tuition..." She stopped and her face lit up. "That's it!"

"What?" I asked.

"You can come to *me* for lessons."

"What sort of lessons?"

She punched my arm. "School lessons, you ninny! You can come round for an hour or two after school every day. I'll help you with your homework and fill you in on stuff you've missed."

"You wouldn't mind?" I asked.

"Of course not," she smiled. "It will be a pleasure."

Enjoyable as the night was, it had to end eventually. I'd forgotten about the possible threat of the vampaneze, but when Debbie excused herself and went to the bathroom, I fell to thinking about them, and wondered if Mr Crepsley or Harkat had sighted any — I didn't want to come to Debbie's for lessons if it meant getting her mixed up in our dangerous affairs.

If I waited for her to return, I might forget about the threat again, so I composed a quick note – 'Have to go. Wonderful to see you. Meet you at school in the morning. Hope you won't mind if I don't do my homework!' – left it on the bare plate which had contained the scones, and ducked out as quietly as possible.

I trotted down the stairs, humming happily, paused outside the main door at the bottom and let rip with three long whistles — my signal to Mr Crepsley to let him know that I was leaving. Then I made my way round to the back of the building and found Harkat hiding behind a couple of large black rubbish bins. "Any trouble?" I asked.

"None," he replied. "Nobody's gone near the place."

Mr Crepsley arrived and crouched behind the bins with us. He looked more solemn than usual. "Spot any vampaneze?" I asked.

"No."

"Mr Tiny?"

"No."

"Things are looking good then," I smiled.

"What about Debbie?" Harkat asked. "Is she on the level?"

"Oh, yes." I gave them a quick account of my conversation with Debbie. Mr Crepsley said nothing, only grunted as I filled him in. He appeared very moody and distant.

"...so we've arranged to meet each evening after school," I finished. "We haven't set a time yet. I wanted to discuss it with you two first, to see if you want to shadow us when we meet. I don't think there's any need – I'm sure Debbie isn't part of a plot – but if you want, we can schedule the lessons for late at night."

Mr Crepsley sighed half-heartedly. "I do not think that will be necessary. I have scouted the area thoroughly. There is no evidence of the vampaneze. It would be preferable if you came in daylight, but not essential."

"Is that a seal of approval?"

"Yes." Again he sounded unusually downhearted.

"What's wrong?" I asked. "You're not still suspicious of Debbie, are you?"

"It has nothing to do with her. I..." He looked at us sadly. "I have bad news."

"Oh?" Harkat and me exchanged uncertain glances.

"Mika Ver Leth transmitted a short telepathic message to me while you were inside."

"Is this about the Lord of the Vampaneze?" I asked nervously.

"No. It is about our friend, your fellow Prince, Paris Skyle. He..." Mr Crepsley sighed again, then said dully, "Paris is dead."

CHAPTER EIGHT

THE DEATH of the ancient Prince should have come as no great surprise — he was the wrong side of eight hundred, the War of the Scars had taken its toll on him, and I remembered thinking when I left Vampire Mountain how poorly he looked — but I hadn't expected him to go this quickly, and the news knocked the wind out of me.

As far as Mr Crepsley knew, the Prince had died of natural causes. He wouldn't be sure until he got to Vampire Mountain — vampires could only send basic telepathic messages — but there'd been no hint of foul play in Mika's message.

I wanted to go with him to the funeral — it would be a huge affair, which almost every vampire in the world would attend — but Mr Crepsley asked me not to. "One Prince must always remain absent from Vampire Mountain," he reminded me, "in case anything happens to the others. I know you were fond of Paris, but Mika, Arrow and Vancha knew him far longer than you. It would be unfair to ask one of them to give up their place."

I was disappointed, but bowed to his wishes — it would have been selfish of me to put myself before the elder Princes. "Tell them to be careful," I warned him. "I don't want to be the only Prince left — if they all perished together, and I had to lead the clan by myself, it would be a disaster!"

"You can say that again," Harkat laughed, but there was no merriment in his voice. "Can I come with you?" he asked Mr Crepsley. "I'd like to pay ... my respects."

"I would rather you remained with Darren," Mr Crepsley said. "I do not like the idea of leaving him on his own."

Harkat nodded immediately. "You're right. I'll stay."

"Thanks," I said softly.

"Now," Mr Crepsley mused, "that leaves us with the question of whether you hold camp here or locate elsewhere."

"We'll stay, of course," I said rather quickly.

Morose as he was, the vampire managed a wry smile. "I thought you would say that. I glimpsed you through the window as you kissed your teacher's cheek."

"You were spying on me!" I huffed.

"That was the general idea, was it not?" he replied. I sputtered indignantly, but of course that *had* been the plan. "You and Harkat should withdraw while I am away," Mr Crepsley continued. "If you come under attack, you will be hard-pushed to defend yourselves."

"I'm ready to risk it if Harkat is," I said.

Harkat shrugged. "The thought of staying doesn't ... frighten me."

"Very well," Mr Crepsley sighed. "But promise me you will abandon the search for the killers while I am absent, and do nothing to endanger yourselves."

"You've no fear on that score," I told him. "Chasing killers is the last thing on my mind. I've something far more terrifying to deal with — homework!"

Mr Crepsley wished us well, then hurried back to the hotel to gather his belongings and depart. He was gone when we got there, probably already at the edge of the city, getting ready to flit. It felt lonely without him, and a little bit scary, but we weren't too worried. He should only be gone a few weeks at most. What could possibly go wrong in so short a time?

The next fortnight was tough. With Mr Crepsley out of the city, the hunt for the vampaneze suspended, and the death count stable (nobody new had been killed recently), I was able to concentrate on school — which was just as well, given the amount of work I had to put into it.

Debbie pulled some strings to lighten my load. Guided by her, I played up the effects of the imaginary fire I'd been trapped in and said I'd missed a lot of school. I explained the good marks by saying my father had been best friends with the headmaster of my old school. Mr Chivers was decidedly unimpressed when he heard that, but Debbie convinced him not to take matters further.

I opted out of modern languages and dropped back a couple of years in maths and science. I felt more peculiar than ever sitting amidst a bunch of thirteen year olds, but at least I was able to follow what they were doing. I still had Mr Smarts for science, but he was more understanding now that he knew I hadn't been faking ignorance, and spent a lot of time helping me catch up.

I faced difficulties in English, history and geography, but with the extra free periods I had instead of languages, I was able to focus on them and was gradually pulling even with the others in my class.

I enjoyed mechanical drawing and computer studies. My Dad had taught me the basics of MD when I was a kid – he'd hoped I'd go into draughtsmanship when I grew up – and I quickly picked up on what I'd missed. To my surprise, I took to computers like a vampire to blood, aided by my super-fast fingers, which could speed about a keyboard faster than any human typist's.

I had to keep a close watch on my powers. I was finding it hard to make friends – my classmates were still suspicious of me – but I knew I could become popular if I took part in the lunchtime sporting activities. I could shine in any game – football, basketball, handball – and everyone likes a winner. The temptation to show off, and earn a few friends in the process, was strong.

But I resisted. The risk was too great. It wasn't just the possibility that I'd do something superhuman – like leap higher than a professional basketball player – which might tip people off to my powers, but the fear that I might injure somebody. If someone dug me in the ribs while playing football, I might lose my temper and take a punch at him, and my punches could put a human in hospital, or worse — a morgue!

PE was therefore a frustrating class — I had to deliberately mask my strength behind a clumsy, pathetic façade. English, oddly enough, was a pain too. It was great to be with Debbie, but when we were in class we had to act like an ordinary teacher and student. There could be no undue familiarity. We maintained a cool, distant air, which made the forty minutes – eighty on Wednesdays and Fridays, when I had double English – pass with agonizing slowness.

After school and at weekends, when I went round to her apartment for private tuition, it was different. There we could relax and discuss whatever we wanted; we could curl up on the couch with a bottle of wine and watch an old film on the TV, or listen to music and chat about the past.

I ate at Debbie's most nights. She loved cooking, and we experimented with a variety of culinary feasts. I soon put on weight, and had to go jogging late at night to keep myself trim.

But it wasn't all relaxation and good food with Debbie. She was determined to educate me to a satisfactory level and spent two or three hours every evening working on my subjects with me. It wasn't easy for her — apart from being tired after her day at work, she didn't know a lot about maths, science and geography — but she stuck with it and set an example which I felt compelled to follow.

"Your grammar's shaky," she said one night, reading through an essay I'd written. "Your English is good but you have some bad habits you need to break."

"Such as?"

"This sentence, for instance: 'John and me went to the store to buy a magazine.' What's wrong with that?"

I thought about it. "We went to buy newspapers?" I suggested innocently.

Debbie threw the copy at me. "Seriously," she giggled.

I picked up the copy and studied the sentence. "It should be 'John and *I*'?" I guessed.

"Yes," she nodded. "You use 'and me' all the time. It's not grammatically correct. You'll have to rise out of it."

"I know," I sighed. "But it'll be tough. I keep a diary, and I've always used 'and me' — it just seems more natural."

"Nobody ever said English was natural," Debbie scolded me, then cocked an eyebrow and added, "I didn't know you kept a diary."

"I've kept one since I was nine years old. All my secrets are in it."

"I hope you don't write about *me*. If it fell into the wrong hands..."

"Hmm," I smirked. "I could blackmail you if I wanted, couldn't I?"

"Just try it," she growled. Then, earnestly, "I really don't think you should write about us, Darren. Or if you do, use a code, or invent a name for me. Diaries *can* be misplaced, and if word of our friendship leaked, I'd have a hard time setting things straight."

"OK. I haven't included any new entries lately – I've been too busy – but when I do, I'll exercise due discretion." That was one of Debbie's pet phrases.

"And make sure when you're describing us that it's 'Miss X and *I*', not 'Miss X and *me*'," she said pompously, then screeched as I pounced across the room and set about tickling her until her face turned red!

CHAPTER NINE

ON MY third Tuesday at school, I made a friend. Richard Montrose was a small, mousey-haired boy, whom I recognized from my English and history classes. He was a year younger than most of the others. He didn't say very much, but was always being complimented by the teachers. Which of course made him the perfect target for bullies.

Since I didn't take part in games on the quad, I spent most of my lunch breaks strolling around, or in the computer room on the third floor of the building at the rear of the school. That's where I was when I heard sounds of a scuffle outside and went to investigate. I found Richard pinned to the wall by Smickey Martin – the guy who'd called me an asswipe on my first day at school – and three of his pals. Smickey was rooting through the younger boy's pockets. "You know you have to pay, Monty," he laughed. "If we don't take yer money, someone else will. Better the devil you know than the devil you don't."

"Please, Smickey," Richard sobbed. "Not this week. I have to buy a new atlas."

"Should have taken more care of your old one," Smickey snickered.

"*You're* the one who ripped it up, you..." Richard was on the point of calling Smickey something awful, but drew up short.

Smickey paused threateningly. "Wot was you gonna call me, Monty?"

"Nothing," Richard gasped, truly frightened now.

"Yes, you was," Smickey snarled. "Hold him, boys. I'm gonna teach him a—"

"You'll teach him nothing," I said quietly from behind.

Smickey turned swiftly. When he saw me, he laughed. "Little Darrsy Horston," he chuckled. "Wot are you doing here?" I didn't answer, only stared coldly at him. "Better run along, Horsty," Smickey said. "We ain't come after you for money yet — but that's not to say we won't!"

"You won't get anything from me," I told him. "And you won't get anything from Richard in future either. Or anyone else."

"Oh?" His eyes narrowed. "Them's awful big words, Horsty. If you take 'em back quick, I might forget you said 'em."

I stepped forward calmly, relishing the chance to put this bully in his place. Smickey frowned — he hadn't been expecting an open challenge — then grinned, grabbed Richard's left arm and swung him towards me. I stepped aside as Richard cried out – I was fully focused on Smickey – but then I heard him collide with something hard. Glancing back, I saw that he'd slammed into the banisters of the stairs and was toppling over — about to fall head first to the floor three storeys below!

I threw myself backwards and snatched for Richard's feet. I missed his left foot but got a couple of fingers on his right ankle just before he disappeared over the side of the handrail. Gripping the fabric of his school trousers hard, I grunted as the weight of his body jerked me roughly against the banisters. There was a ripping sound, and I feared his trousers would tear and I'd lose him. But the material held, and as he hung over the railings, whimpering, I hauled him back up and set him on his feet.

When Richard was safe, I turned to deal with Smickey Martin and the rest, but they'd scattered like the cowards they were. "So much for that lot," I muttered, then asked Richard if he was OK. He nodded feebly but said nothing. I left him where he was and returned to the soft hum of the computer room.

Moments later, Richard appeared in the doorway. He was still shaking, but he was smiling also. "You saved my life," he said. I shrugged and stared at the screen as though immersed in it. Richard waited a few seconds, then said, "Thanks."

"No problem." I glanced up at him. "Three floors isn't that big a fall. You'd probably only have broken a few bones."

"I don't think so," Richard said. "I was going nose-down, like a plane." He sat beside me and studied the screen. "Creating a screen saver?"

"Yes."

"I know where to find some really good scenes from sci-fi and horror movies. Want me to show you?"

I nodded. "That'd be cool."

Smiling, his fingers flew over the keyboard and soon we were discussing school and homework and computers, and the rest of the lunch break whizzed by.

Richard swapped seats in English and history in order to sit beside me, and let me copy from his notes — he had his own shorthand system which allowed him to jot down everything that was said in class. He also started spending most of his breaks and lunches with me. He pulled me out of the computer room and introduced me to other friends of his. They didn't exactly welcome me with open arms, but at least I had a few people to talk to now.

It was fun hanging out, discussing TV, comics, music, books and (of course!) girls. Harkat and me — Harkat and *I* — had TV sets in our rooms at the hotel, and I started watching a few programmes at night. Most of the stuff my new friends enjoyed was formulaic and tedious, but I pretended to enthuse about it like they did.

The week passed swiftly and before I knew it I was facing another weekend. For the first time I was mildly disappointed to have two free days on my hands – Richard would be away at his grandparents' – but cheered up at the thought of spending them with Debbie.

I'd been thinking a lot about Debbie, and the bond between us. We'd been very close as teenagers, and I now felt closer to her than ever. I knew there were obstacles — especially my appearance — but having spent so much time with her, I now believed we could overcome those obstacles and pick up where we'd left off thirteen years before.

That Friday night, I summoned all my courage as we were sitting together on the couch, leant over and tried to kiss Debbie. She looked surprised, and pushed me away lightly, laughing uneasily. When I tried to kiss her again, her surprise turned to icy anger and she shoved me away firmly. "No!" she snapped.

"Why not?" I retorted, upset.

"I'm your teacher," Debbie said, standing. "You're my student. It wouldn't be right."

"I don't want to be your student," I growled, standing up beside her. "I want to be your boyfriend."

I leant forward to kiss her again, but before I could, she slapped me hard. I blinked and stared at her, stunned. She slapped me again, softer this time. She was trembling and there were tears in her eyes.

"Debbie," I groaned, "I didn't mean to—"

"I want you to leave now," Debbie said. I took a couple of steps back, then halted. I opened my mouth to protest. "No," Debbie said. "Don't say anything. Just go, please."

Nodding miserably, I turned my back on her and walked to the door. I paused with my fingers on the handle and spoke to her without looking back. "I only wanted to be closer to you. I didn't mean any harm."

After short silence Debbie sighed and said, "I know."

I risked a quick look back — Debbie had her arms crossed over her chest and was gazing down at the floor. She was close to crying. "Does this change things between us?" I asked.

"I don't know," she answered honestly. She glanced up at me and I could see confusion mingled in her eyes with the tears. "Let's leave it for a couple of days. We'll talk about this on Monday. I need to think it over."

"OK." I opened the door, took a step out, then said very quickly, "You might not want to hear this, but I love you, Debbie. I love you more than anybody else in the world." Before she could reply, I shut the door and slunk away down the stairs like a downtrodden rat.

CHAPTER TEN

I PACED the streets as though walking fast could rid me of my problems, thinking of things I might have said to Debbie to make her accept me. I was sure she felt the same way about me that I felt about her. But my looks were confusing her. I had to find a way to get her to view me as an adult, not a child. What if I told her the truth? I imagined breaking the news to her:

"Debbie, prepare yourself for a shock — I'm a vampire."

"That's nice, dear."

"You're not upset?"

"Should I be?"

"I drink blood! I creep around in the dead of night, find sleeping humans, and open up their veins!"

"Well ... nobody's perfect."

The imaginary conversation brought a fleeting smile to my lips. Actually, I had no idea how Debbie would react. I'd never broken the news to a human before. I didn't know where or how to start, or what a person would say in response. *I* knew vampires weren't the murderous, emotionless monsters of horror movies and books — but how would I convince others?

"Bloody humans!" I grumbled, kicking a postbox in anger. "Bloody vampires! We should all be turtles or something!"

On that ridiculous thought, I looked around and realized I'd no idea which part of city I was in. I scouted for a familiar street name, so I could chart a course for home. The streets were largely deserted. Now that the mystery killers had stopped or moved on, the soldiers had withdrawn, and although local police still patrolled the streets, the barricades had come down and you could walk unheeded. Even so, the curfew was still in effect, and most people were happy to respect it.

I relished the dark, quiet streets. Walking alone down narrow, twisting alleys, I could have been winding my way through the tunnels of Vampire Mountain. It was comforting to imagine myself back with Seba Nile, Vanez Blane and the others, no love life, school or fate-fuelled quests to trouble me.

Thinking about Vampire Mountain set me thinking about Paris Skyle. I'd been so busy with school and Debbie, I hadn't had time to brood on the death of the Prince. I'd miss the old vampire who'd taught me so much. We'd shared laughter as well. As I stepped over a pile of rubbish strewn across the ground of a particularly dark alley, I recalled the time a few years ago when he leant too close to a candle and set his beard on fire. He'd hopped around the Hall of Princes like a clown, shrieking and slapping at the flames until—

Something struck the back of my head, hard, and I went toppling into the rubbish. I cried out as I fell, my recollections of Paris shattering, then rolled away defensively, clutching my head between my hands. As I rolled, a silver object came crashing down on the ground where my head had been, and sparks flew.

Ignoring my wounded head, I scrambled to my knees and looked for something to defend myself with. The plastic top of a dustbin lay nearby. It wouldn't be much good but it was all I could find. Stooping swiftly, I snatched it up and held it in front of me like a shield, turning to meet the charge of my assailant, who was streaking towards me at a speed no human could have matched.

Something gold flashed and swung down upon my makeshift shield, cutting the dustbin lid in half. Somebody chuckled, and it was the sound of pure, insane evil.

For a dreadful moment I thought it was Murlough's ghost, come to wreak revenge. But that was silly. I believed in ghosts – Harkat used to be one, before Mr Tiny brought him back from the dead – but this guy was far too solid to be a spirit.

"I'll cut you to pieces!" my attacker boasted, circling me warily. There was something familiar about his voice, but try as I might, I couldn't place it.

I studied his outline as he circled around me. He was wearing dark clothes and his face was masked by a balaclava. The ends of a beard jutted out from underneath it. He was large and chunky – but not as fat as Murlough had been – and I could see two blood-red eyes glinting above his snarling teeth. He had no hands, just two metallic attachments – one gold, the other silver – attached to the ends of his elbows. There were three hooks on each attachment, sharp, curved and deadly.

The vampaneze – the eyes and speed were the giveaway – struck. He was fast, but I avoided the killer hooks, which dug into the wall behind me and gouged out a sizeable crater when he pulled free. It took less than a second for my attacker to free his hand, but I used that time to strike, kicking him in the chest. But he'd been expecting it and brought his other arm down upon my shin, cruelly knocking my leg aside.

I yelped as pain shot up the length of my leg. Hopping madly, I threw the two halves of the useless dustbin lid at the vampaneze. He ducked out of the way, laughing. I tried to run — no good. My injured leg wouldn't support me, and after a couple of strides I collapsed to the floor, helpless.

I whirled over on to my back and stared up at the hook-handed vampaneze as he took his time approaching. He swung his arms back and forth as he got closer, the hooks making horrible screeching noises as they scraped together. "Going to cut you," the vampaneze hissed. "Slow and painful. I'll start on your fingers. Slice them off, one at a time. Then your hands. Then your toes. Then–"

There was a sharp clicking noise, followed by the hiss of parted air. Something shot by the vampaneze's head, only narrowly missing. It struck the wall and embedded itself — a short, thick, steel-tipped arrow. The vampaneze cursed and crouched, hiding in the shadows of the alley.

Moments ticked by like spiders scuttling up my spine. The vampaneze's angry breath and my gasping sobs filled the air. There was no sight or sound of the person who'd fired the arrow. Shuffling backwards, the vampaneze locked gazes with me and bared his teeth. "I'll get you later," he vowed. "You'll die slowly, in great agony. I'll cut you. Fingers first. One at a time." Then he turned and sprinted. A second arrow was fired after him, but he ducked low and again it missed, burying itself in a large bag of rubbish. The vampaneze exploded out of the end of the alley and vanished quickly into the night.

There was a lengthy pause. Then footsteps. A man of medium height appeared out of the gloom. He was dressed in black, with a long scarf looped around his neck, and gloves covering his hands. He had grey hair — though he wasn't old — and there was a stern set to his features. He was holding a gun-shaped weapon, out of the end of which jutted a steel-tipped arrow. Another of the arrow-firing guns was slung over his left shoulder.

I sat up, grunting, and tried to rub some life back into my right leg. "Thanks," I said as the man got closer. He didn't answer, just proceeded to the end of the alley, where he scanned the area beyond for signs of the vampaneze.

Turning, the grey-haired man came back and stopped a couple of metres away. He was holding the arrow gun in his right hand, but it wasn't pointed harmlessly down at the ground — it was pointing at *me*.

"Mind lowering that?" I asked, forcing a sheepish smile. "You just saved my life. Be a shame if that went off by accident and killed me."

He didn't reply immediately. Nor did he lower the gun. There was no warmth in his expression. "Does it surprise you that I spared your life?" he asked. As with the vampaneze, there was something familiar about this man's voice, but again I couldn't place it.

"I ... guess," I said weakly, nervously eyeing the arrow gun.

"Do you know why I saved you?"

I gulped. "Out of the goodness of your heart?"

"Maybe." He took a step closer. The tip of the gun was now aimed directly at my heart. If he fired, he'd create a hole the size of a football in my chest. "Or maybe I was saving you for myself!" he hissed.

"Who are you?" I croaked, desperately pressing back against the wall.

"You don't recognize me?"

I shook my head. I was certain I'd seen his face before, but I couldn't put a name to it.

The man breathed out through his nose. "Strange. I never thought you'd forget. Then again, it's been a long time, and the years haven't been as kind to me as they've been to you. Perhaps you'll remember *this*." He held out his left hand. The palm of the glove had been cut away, exposing the flesh beneath. It was an ordinary hand in all respects save one — in the centre, a rough cross had been carved into the flesh.

As I stared at the cross, pink and tender-looking, the years evaporated and I was back in a cemetery on my first night as a vampire's assistant, facing a boy whose life I'd saved, a boy who was jealous of me, who thought I'd conspired with Mr Crepsley and betrayed him.

"*Steve!*" I gasped, staring from the cross to his cold, hard eyes. "*Steve Leopard!*"

"Yes," he nodded grimly.

Steve Leopard, my one-time best friend. The angry, mixed-up boy who'd sworn to become a vampire hunter when he grew up, so that he could track me down — and kill me!

CHAPTER ELEVEN

HE WAS close enough for me to lunge at the gun barrel and maybe redirect it. But I couldn't move. I was stunned beyond anything but passive observation. Debbie Hemlock walking into my English class had left me gobsmacked — but Steve Leopard (his real name was Leonard) turning up out of the blue like this was ten times as shocking.

After a handful of anxious seconds, Steve lowered the arrow gun, then jammed it through a belt behind his back. He extended his hands, took my left arm above the elbow, and hauled me to my feet. I rose obediently, a puppet in his hands.

"Had you going for a minute, didn't I?" he said — and smiled.

"You're not going to kill me?" I wheezed.

"Hardly!" He took my right hand and shook it awkwardly. "Hello, Darren. Good to see you again, old friend."

I stared at our clasped hands, then at his face. Then I threw my arms around him and hugged him for dear life. "Steve!" I sobbed into his shoulder.

"Stop that," he muttered and I could hear the sound of his own voice breaking. "You'll have *me* in tears if you keep it up." Pushing me away, he wiped around his eyes and grinned.

I dried my cheeks and beamed. "It's really you!"

"Of course. You don't think two people could be born this handsome, do you?"

"Modest as ever," I noted wryly.

"Nothing to be modest about," he sniffed, then laughed. "You able to walk?"

"I think a hobble's the best I can manage," I said.

"Then lean on me. I don't want to hang around. Hooky might come back with his friends."

"*Hooky*? Oh, you mean the vampa—" I stopped, wondering how much Steve knew about the creatures of the night.

"The vampaneze," he finished, nodding soberly.

"You know about them?"

"Obviously."

"Is the hook-handed guy the one who's been killing people?"

"Yes. But he isn't alone. We'll discuss it later. Let's get you out of here and cleaned up first." Letting me lean on him, Steve led me back the way I'd come, and as we walked I couldn't help wondering if I'd been knocked unconscious in the alley. If not for the pain in my leg – which was all too real — I'd have been seriously tempted to think this was nothing but a wishful dream.

Steve took me to the fifth floor of a run-down apartment block. Many of the doors we passed along the landing were boarded-over or broken down. "Nice neighbourhood," I commented sarcastically.

"It's a condemned building," he said. "A few apartments are occupied — mostly by old folk with nowhere else to go — but the majority are empty. I prefer places like this to boarding houses and hotels. The space and quiet suit my purposes."

Steve stopped at a battered brown door kept shut by an extra thick padlock and chain. Rooting through his pockets, he found a key, unlocked the padlock, removed the chain and pushed the door open. The air inside was stale, but he took no notice as he bundled me inside and closed the door. The darkness within held until he lit a candle. "No electricity," he said. "The lower apartments are still connected, but it went off up here last week."

He helped me into a cluttered living room and laid me down on a couch that had seen better days — it was threadbare, and wiry springs stuck out through several holes. "Try not to impale yourself," Steve laughed.

"Is your interior decorator on strike?" I asked.

"Don't complain," Steve scolded me. "It's a good base to work from. If we had to report back to some swanky hotel, we'd have to explain your leg and why we're covered in filth.

As for accounting for *these*..." He shrugged off the pair of arrow guns and laid them down.

"Care to tell me what's going on, Steve?" I asked quietly. "How you were in that alley and why you're carrying those?"

"Later," he said, "after we've tended to your wounds. And after you've—" he produced a mobile phone and tossed it to me "—made a call."

"Who am I supposed to ring?" I asked, staring at the phone suspiciously.

"Hooky followed you from your friend's house — the dark-skinned lady."

My face whitened. "He knows where Debbie lives?" I gasped.

"If that's her name — yes. I doubt he'll go after her, but if you don't want to run the risk, my advice is to call and tell her to—"

I was hitting buttons before he finished. Debbie's phone rang four times. Five. Six. Seven. I was about to dash to her rescue, regardless of my bad leg, when she picked up and said, "Hello?"

"It's me."

"Darren? What are—"

"Debbie — do you trust me?"

There was a startled pause. "Is this a joke?"

"Do you trust me?" I growled.

"Of course," she answered, sensing my seriousness.

"Then get out now. Throw some gear into a bag and scram. Find a hotel for the weekend. Stay there."

"Darren, what's going on? Have you lost your—"

"Do you want to die?" I interrupted.

A silent beat. Then, quietly, "No."

"Then get out." I hit the disconnect button and prayed she'd heed my warning. "Does the vampaneze know where I'm staying?" I asked, thinking of Harkat.

"I doubt it," Steve said. "If he did, he'd have attacked you there. From what I saw, he stumbled upon you earlier tonight by chance. He was casing a crowd, selecting his next victim, when he saw you and picked up your trail. He followed you to your friend's house, waited, trailed after you when you left, and..."

I knew the rest.

Steve fetched a first-aid kit from a shelf behind the couch. He told me to lean forward, then examined the back of my head. "Is it cut?" I asked.

"Yes, but not badly. It doesn't need stitches. I'll clean it up and apply a dressing." With my head seen to, he focused on my leg. It was deeply gashed and the material of my trousers was soaked through with blood. Steve snipped it away with a sharp pair of scissors, exposing the flesh beneath, then swabbed at the wound with cotton wool. When it was clean, he studied it momentarily, then left and came back with a reel of catgut and a needle. "This'll hurt," he said.

"It won't be the first time I've been stitched back together," I grinned. He went to work on the cut, and did a neat job on it. I'd only have a small scar when it was fully healed. "You've done this before," I noted as he tucked the catgut away.

"I took first-aid classes," he said. "Figured they'd come in handy. Never guessed who my first patient would be." He asked if I wanted something to drink.

"Just some water."

He pulled a bottle of mineral water out of a bag by the sink and filled a couple of glasses. "Sorry it's not cold. The fridge won't work without electricity."

"No problem," I said, taking a long drink. Then I nodded at the sink. "Has the water been cut off too?"

"No, but you wouldn't want to drink any — fine for washing, but you'd be on a toilet for days if you swallowed."

We smiled at each other over the rims of our glasses.

"So," I said, "mind telling me what you've been up to these last fifteen years?"

"You first," Steve said.

"Nuh-uh. You're the host. It's your place to start."

"Toss you for it?" he suggested.

"OK."

He produced a coin and told me to call. "Heads."

He flipped the coin, caught it and slapped it over. When he took his hand away he grimaced. "I never did have much luck," he sighed, then started to talk. It was a long story, and we were down to the bottom of the bottle of water and on to a second candle before he finished.

Steve hated Mr Crepsley and me for a long, long time. He'd sit up late into the night, plotting his future, dreaming of the day he'd track us down and stake us through the heart. "I was crazy with rage," he muttered. "I couldn't think about anything else. In woodwork classes I made stakes. In geography I committed the maps of the world to memory, so I'd know my way around whichever country I traced you to."

He found out everything there was to know about vampires. He'd had a large collection of horror books when I knew him, but he'd doubled, then trebled that in the space of a year. He learnt what climates we favoured, where we preferred to make our homes, how best to kill us. "I got in contact with people on the Internet," he said. "You'd be surprised how many vampire hunters there are. We exchanged notes, stories, opinions. Most were crackpots, but a few knew what they were talking about."

When he turned sixteen he left school and home, and went out into the world. He supported himself through a series of odd jobs, working in hotels, restaurants and factories. Sometimes he stole, or broke into empty houses and squatted. They were rough, lean, lonely years. He had very few scruples, hardly any friends, and no real interests except learning how to become a killer of vampires.

"To begin with, I thought I'd pretend to befriend them," he explained. "I went in search of vampires, acting as if I wanted to become one. Most of what I'd read in books or gleaned through the Internet was rubbish. I decided the best way to rid myself of my enemies was to get to know them."

Of course, when he eventually tracked a few vampires down and worked himself into their good books, he realized we weren't monsters. He discovered our respect for life, that we didn't kill humans when we drank and that we were people of honour. "It made me take a long, hard look at myself," he sighed, his face dark and sad by the light of the candle. "I saw that *I* was the monster, like Captain Ahab in *Moby Dick*, chasing a pair of killer whales — except these whales weren't killers!"

Gradually his hatred subsided. He still resented me for going off with Mr Crepsley, but accepted the fact that I hadn't done it to spite him. When he looked back at the past, he saw that I'd given up my family and home to save his life, and hadn't tricked or plotted against him.

That's when he dropped his crazy quest. He stopped searching for us, put all thoughts of revenge from his mind, and sat down to work out what he was going to do with the rest of his life. "I could have gone back," he said. "My mother's still alive. I could have returned home, finished my education, found a normal job, carved out an ordinary life for myself. But the night has a way of claiming those who embrace it. I'd found out the truth about vampires — but also about vampaneze."

Steve couldn't stop thinking about the vampaneze. He thought it was incredible that creatures like that could exist, roaming and killing as they pleased. It angered him. He wanted to put a stop to their murderous ways. "But I couldn't go to the police," he smiled ruefully. "I'd have had to capture a live vampaneze to prove they existed, but taking a vampaneze alive is almost impossible, as I'm sure you know.

Even if they believed me, what could they have done? Vampaneze move in, kill, then move on. By the time I'd convinced the police of the danger they were in, the vampaneze would have vanished, and the danger with him. There was only one thing for it — I had to take them on myself!"

Applying the knowledge he'd gathered when studying to be a vampire hunter, Steve set himself the task of tracking down and killing as many vampaneze as he could. It wasn't easy — vampaneze hide their tracks (and the bodies of their victims) expertly, leaving little evidence of their existence — but in time he found people who knew something of their ways, and he built up a picture of vampaneze habits, traits and routes, and eventually stumbled upon one.

"Killing him was the hardest thing I'd ever done," Steve said grimly. "I knew he was a killer, and would kill again if I let him go, but as I stood there, studying him while he slept..." He shivered.

"How did you do it?" I asked quietly. "A stake?"

He nodded bitterly. "Fool that I was — yes."

"I don't understand," I frowned. "Isn't a stake the best way to kill a vampaneze, like with vampires?"

He stared coldly at me. "Ever kill anybody with a stake?"

"No."

"Don't!" he snorted. "Driving it in is simple enough, but blood gushes up into your face, over your arms and chest, and the vampaneze doesn't die straightaway like vampires do in movies. The one I killed lived for the better part of a minute, thrashing and screaming. He crawled out of the coffin and came after me. He was slow, but I slipped on his blood, and before I knew what was happening, he was on top of me."

"What did you do?" I gasped.

"I punched and kicked him and tried to knock him off. Fortunately he'd lost too much blood and hadn't the strength to kill me. But he died on top of me, his blood drenching me, his face next to mine as he shuddered and sobbed and..."

Steve looked away. I didn't press him for further details.

"Since then I've learnt to use those." He nodded at the arrow guns. "They're the best there is. An axe is good too – if you have a good aim and the strength to chop a head clean off — but stay away from ordinary guns — they're not reliable where the extra tough bones and muscles of the vampaneze are concerned."

"I'll bear that in mind," I said, grinning sickly, then asked how many vampaneze Steve had killed.

"Six, though two of those were mad and would have died before long anyway."

I was impressed. "That's more than most vampires kill."

"Humans have an advantage over vampires," Steve said. "We can move about and strike by day. In a fair contest, a vampaneze would wipe the floor with me. But if you catch them in the day, while they're sleeping...

"Although," he added, "that's changing. The last few I've tracked have been accompanied by humans. I wasn't able to get close enough to kill them. It's the first time I've heard of vampaneze travelling with human assistants."

"They're called vampets," I told him.

He frowned. "How do you know? I thought the families of the night had nothing to do with one another."

"We hadn't until recently," I said grimly, then glanced at my watch. Steve's story wasn't complete — he still hadn't explained how he'd wound up here — but it was time I made a move. It was getting late and I didn't want Harkat to worry. "Will you come to my hotel with me? You can finish telling me about yourself there. Besides, there's someone I'd like you to share your story with."

"Mr Crepsley?" Steve guessed.

"No. He's away on ... business. This is somebody else."

"Who?"

"It would take too long to explain. Will you come?"

He hesitated a moment, then said he would. But he stopped to grab his arrow guns before we left — I had a feeling Steve didn't even go to the toilet without his weapons!

CHAPTER TWELVE

DURING THE walk to the hotel, I filled Steve in on what I'd been up to. It was a greatly condensed version, but I covered most of the bases, and told him about the War of the Scars and how it started.

"The Lord of the Vampaneze," he muttered. "I thought it was strange, how they were organizing."

I asked Steve about my family and friends, but he hadn't been home since he was sixteen, and knew nothing about them.

At the hotel he clambered on to my back and I scaled the outside wall. The stitches in my leg strained with the effort, but held. I rapped on the window and Harkat quickly appeared and let us in. He stared suspiciously at Steve but said nothing until I'd made the introductions.

"Steve Leopard," he mused. "I've heard much ... about you."

"None of it good, I bet," Steve laughed, rubbing his hands together — he hadn't taken off his gloves, although he'd loosened his scarf slightly. There was a strong medicinal smell coming from him, which I only noticed now that we were in a warm, normal room.

"What's he doing here?" Harkat asked me, green eyes pinned on Steve. I gave him a quick run-down. Harkat relaxed slightly when he heard that Steve had saved my life, but remained on guard. "You think it was wise to bring ... him here?"

"He's my friend," I said shortly. "He saved my life."

"But he knows where we are now."

"So?" I snapped.

"Harkat's right," Steve said. "I'm human. If I fell into the hands of the vampaneze, they could torture the name of this place out of me. You should move on to somewhere new in the morning, and not tell me about it."

"I don't think that will be necessary," I said stiffly, angry with Harkat for not trusting Steve.

There was an uncomfortable silence. "Well!" Steve laughed, breaking it. "It's rude to ask, but I have to. What on earth *are* you, Harkat Mulds?"

The Little Person grinned at the directness of the question and warmed to Steve a bit. Asking Steve to sit, he told him about himself, how he was a ghost who'd been brought back to life by Mr Tiny. Steve was astounded. "I've never heard anything like this before!" he exclaimed. "I was interested in the small people in the blue robes when I saw them at the Cirque Du Freak — I sensed there was something weird about them. But with all that's happened since, they'd slipped my mind entirely."

Harkat's revelation – that he'd been a ghost – unnerved Steve. "Something wrong?" I asked.

"Kind of," he muttered. "I never believed in life after death. When I killed, I thought that was the end of the matter. Knowing that people have souls, that they can survive death and even come back... It's not the most welcome news."

"Afraid the vampaneze you killed will come after you?" I smirked.

"Something like that." Shaking his head, Steve settled down and finished telling the story he'd started earlier that night in his apartment. "I came here two months ago, when I heard reports of what appeared to be a vampaneze presence. I thought the killer must be a mad vampaneze, since normally only the crazy ones leave bodies where they can be found. But what I discovered was far more disturbing."

Steve was a highly resourceful investigator. He'd managed to examine three of the victims, and found minor differences in the ways they'd been killed. "Vampaneze – even the crazy ones – have highly developed drinking patterns. No two kill and drain a victim exactly alike, and no vampaneze varies his method. There had to be more than one of them at work."

And since mad vampaneze were by their nature loners, Steve concluded that the killers must be sane.

"But it doesn't make sense," he sighed. "Sane vampaneze shouldn't leave bodies where they can be found. As far as I can figure, they're setting a trap for someone, though I've no idea who."

I glanced questioningly at Harkat. He hesitated, then nodded. "Tell him," he said, and I told Steve about the fake forms which had been sent to Mahler's.

"They're after *you*?" Steve asked incredulously.

"Possibly," I said. "Or Mr Crepsley. But we're not entirely sure. Somebody else might be behind it, someone who wants to pit us against the vampaneze."

Steve thought about that in silence.

"You still haven't told us how you were ... there to save Darren tonight," Harkat said, interrupting Steve's reverie.

Steve shrugged. "Luck. I've been turning this city upside-down, searching for vampaneze. The killers aren't in any of their usual hiding places — abandoned factories or buildings, crypts, old theatres. Eight nights ago, I spotted a large man with hooks for hands emerging from an underground tunnel."

"That's the guy who attacked me," I told Harkat. "He has three hooks on either arm. One hand's made of gold, the other of silver."

"I've been following him every night since," Steve continued. "It isn't easy for a human to trail a vampaneze — their senses are much more acute — but I've had plenty of practice. Sometimes I lose him, but I always pick him up again exiting the tunnels at dusk."

"He comes out the same way every night?" I asked.

"Of course not," Steve snorted. "Even a crazy vampaneze wouldn't do that."

"Then how do you find him?"

"By wiring manhole covers." Steve beamed proudly. "Vampaneze won't use the same exit night after night, but they tend to stick to a strictly defined area when they set up base. I wired every manhole cover within a two hundred metre radius — I've extended that to half a kilometre since. Whenever one of them opens, a light flashes on a kit I have, and it's a simple matter to track the vampaneze down.

"At least, it *was*." He paused unhappily. "After tonight, he'll probably move on to somewhere new. He won't know how much I know about him, but he'll expect the worst. I don't think he'll use those tunnels again."

"Did you know it was Darren you were saving?" Harkat asked.

Steve nodded seriously. "I wouldn't have come to his rescue otherwise."

"What do you mean?" I frowned.

"I could have taken Hooky out ages ago," Steve said, "but I knew he wasn't working alone. I wanted to track down his companions. I've been exploring the tunnels by day, hoping to trail him to his base. By interfering tonight, I've blown that chance. I wouldn't have done that for anyone but you."

"If he'd attacked an ordinary human, you'd have let him kill?" I gasped.

"Yes." Steve's eyes were hard. "If sacrificing one person means saving many more, I will. If I hadn't caught a glimpse of your face as you left your lady friend's, I'd have let Hooky kill you."

That was a harsh way of looking at the world, but it was a way I understood. Vampires knew the needs of the group had to be put before those of the individual. It surprised me that Steve was able to think that way — most humans can't — but I suppose you have to learn to be ruthless if you dedicate yourself to the hunting and killing of ruthless creatures.

"That's about the bones of it," Steve said, pulling his dark overcoat a notch tighter around his shoulders, suppressing a shiver. "There's plenty I haven't mentioned, but I've covered most of the major stuff."

"Are you cold?" Harkat asked, noting Steve's shivers. "I can turn up the heat."

"Wouldn't do any good," Steve said. "I picked up some kind of germ when Mr Crepsley *tested* me all those years ago. I catch colds simply by looking at someone with a runny nose." He plucked at the scarf around his throat, then wiggled his gloved fingers. "That's why I wrap up so much. If I don't, I wind up confined to bed for days on ends, coughing and spluttering."

"Is that why you smell?" I asked.

Steve laughed. "Yeah. It's a special herbal mix. I rub it in all over before I get dressed every morning. It works wonders. The only drawback is the stench. I have to be careful to keep downwind of the vampaneze when I'm tracking them — one whiff of this and they'd have me pegged."

We discussed the past some more — Steve wanted to know what life in the Cirque Du Freak had been like; I wanted to know where he'd been and what he'd got up to when he wasn't hunting — then talk returned to the present and what we were going to do about the vampaneze.

"If Hooky was acting alone," Steve said, "my attack would have driven him off. The vampaneze don't take chances when they're alone. If they think they've been discovered, they flee. But since he's part of a gang, I doubt he'll run."

"I agree," I said. "They've gone to too much trouble preparing this trap to walk away the first time something goes wrong."

"Do you think the vampaneze will know it was ... you who saved Darren?" Harkat asked.

"I don't see how," Steve replied. "They know nothing about me. They'll probably think it was you or Mr Crepsley. I was careful not to reveal myself to Hooky."

"Then we might still get the better of them," Harkat said. "We haven't gone hunting for them since ... Mr Crepsley left. It would be too dangerous, just the ... two of us."

"But if you had *me* to go with you," Steve said, reading Harkat's thoughts, "it would be different. I'm accustomed to vampaneze hunts. I know where to look and how to track them."

"And with us to back you up," I added, "you could work faster than normal and cover more ground."

We gazed silently around at one another.

"You'd be taking a big risk, getting involved ... with us," Harkat warned him. "Whoever set us up knows all ... about us. You might tip them off to your presence by ... pitching in with us."

"It'd be risky for you too," Steve countered. "You're safe up here. Underground, it's their turf, and if we go down, we're inviting an attack. Remember — though vampaneze usually sleep by day, they don't need to when they're sheltered from the sun. They could be awake and waiting."

We thought about it some more. Then I stretched forth my right hand and held it out in front of me, palm downwards. "I'm up for it if you are," I said.

Steve immediately laid his left hand – the one with the scarred palm – on top of mine and said, "I've nothing to lose. I'm with you."

Harkat was slower to react. "I wish Mr Crepsley was here," he mumbled.

"Me too," I said. "But he's not. And the longer we wait for him, the more time the vampaneze have to plan an attack. If Steve's right, and they panic and switch base, it'll take them a while to settle. They'll be vulnerable. This could be our best chance to strike."

Harkat sighed unhappily. "It could also be our best chance to walk ... straight into a trap. But," he added, laying a large grey hand on top of ours, "the rewards justify the risks. If we can find and kill them, we'll save ... many lives. I'm with you."

Smiling at Harkat, I proposed a vow. "To the death?" I suggested.

"To the death," Steve agreed.

"To the death," Harkat nodded, then added pointedly, "but not, I hope, *ours!*"

CHAPTER THIRTEEN

WE SPENT Saturday and Sunday exploring the tunnels. Harkat and Steve carried arrow guns. They were simple to use — load an arrow, point and fire. Deadly up to a range of twenty metres. As a vampire, I'd sworn not to use such weapons, so I had to make do with my usual short sword and knives.

We started with the area where Steve had first spotted 'Hooky', in the hope of finding some trace of him or his companions. We took the tunnels one at a time, examining the walls for marks of vampaneze nails or hooks, listening carefully for sounds of life, keeping within sight of each other. We moved swiftly at first — Steve knew these tunnels — but when our search extended to new, unfamiliar sections, we advanced more cautiously.

We found nothing.

That night, after a long wash and simple meal together, we talked some more. Steve hadn't changed much. He was as lively and funny as ever, although he'd sometimes get a faraway look in his eyes and fall silent, perhaps thinking about the vampaneze he'd killed or the path in life he'd chosen. He got nervous whenever talk swung round to Mr Crepsley. Steve had never forgotten the vampire's reason for rejecting him – Mr Crepsley said Steve had bad blood and was evil – and didn't think the vampire would be glad to see him.

"I don't know why he thought I was evil," Steve grumbled. "I was wild as a kid, sure, but never evil — was I, Darren?"

"Of course not," I said.

"Maybe he mistook determination for evil," Steve mused. "When I believe in a cause, I'll commit to it wholeheartedly. Like my quest to kill vampaneze. Most humans couldn't kill another living being, even a killer. They'd rather turn them over to the law. But I'll go on killing vampaneze until I die. Maybe Mr Crepsley saw my *ability* to kill and confused it with a *desire* to kill."

We had lots of dark conversations like that, talking about the human soul and the nature of good and evil. Steve had devoted many long hours to Mr Crepsley's cruel judgement. He was almost obsessed with it. "I can't wait to prove him wrong," he smiled. "When he learns I'm on his side, helping the vampires in spite of his rejecting me... That's something I'm looking forward to."

When the weekend drew to a close, I had a decision to make regarding school. I didn't want to bother with Mahler's – it seemed a waste of time – but there was Debbie and Mr

Blaws to consider. If I dropped out suddenly, without a reason, the inspector would come looking for me. Steve said this wasn't a problem, that we could switch to another hotel, but I didn't want to leave until Mr Crepsley returned. The Debbie situation was even more complicated. The vampaneze now knew she was connected to me, and where she lived. Somehow I had to convince her to move to a new apartment — but how? What sort of a story could I concoct to persuade her to leave home?

I decided to go to school that Monday morning, mostly to sort things out with Debbie. With my other teachers, I'd pretend I was coming down with a virus, so they wouldn't suspect anything was amiss when I didn't turn up the next day. I didn't think Mr Blaws would be sent to investigate before the weekend — missing three or four days was hardly unusual — and by the time he did, Mr Crepsley would have hopefully returned. When he was back, we could sit down and establish a definite plan.

Steve and Harkat were going to continue hunting for the vampaneze when I was at school, but agreed to be careful, and promised not to engage them by themselves if they found any.

At Mahler's, I looked for Debbie before classes began. I was going to tell her that an enemy from my past had found out I was seeing her, and I feared he planned to hurt her, to get at me. I'd say he didn't know where she worked, just where she lived, so if she found somewhere new for a few weeks and didn't go back to her old apartment, she'd be fine.

It was a weak story, but I could think of nothing better. I'd plead with her if I had to, and do all in my power to persuade her to heed my warning. If that failed, I'd have to consider kidnapping her and locking her up to protect her.

But there was no sign of Debbie at school. I went to the staffroom during the break, but she hadn't turned up for work and nobody knew where she was. Mr Chivers was with the teachers and he was furious. He couldn't stand it when people – teachers or students – didn't call in before going absent.

I returned to class with a sinking feeling in my gut. I wished I'd asked Debbie to contact me with her new address, but hadn't thought of that when I'd told her to move. Now there was no way for me to check on her.

The two hours of classes and first forty minutes of lunch were some of the most miserable moments of my life. I wanted to flee the school and dash round to Debbie's old apartment, to see if there was any sign of her there. But I realized that it would be better not to act at all than to act in panic. It was tearing me apart, but it would be for the best if I waited for my head to clear before I went investigating.

Then, at ten to two, something wonderful happened — Debbie arrived! I was moping about in the computer room – Richard had sensed my dark mood and left me alone – when I saw her pulling up outside the back of the school in a car accompanied by two men and a woman — all three dressed in police uniforms! Getting out, she entered the building with the woman and one of the men.

Hurrying, I caught up with her on her way to Mr Chivers' office. "Miss Hemlock!" I shouted, alarming the policeman, who turned quickly, hand going for a weapon on his belt. He stopped when he saw my school uniform and relaxed. I raised a shaking hand. "Could I talk to you for a minute, Miss?"

Debbie asked the officers if she could have a few words with me. They nodded, but kept a close watch on us. "What's going on?" I whispered.

"You don't know?" She'd been crying and her face was a mess. I shook my head. "Why did you tell me to leave?" she asked, and there was surprising bitterness in her voice.

"It's complicated."

"Did you know what was going to happen? If you did, I'll hate you forever!"

"Debbie, I don't know what you're talking about. Honestly."

She studied my face for a hint of a lie. Finding none, her expression softened. "You'll hear about it on the news soon," she muttered, "so I guess it doesn't matter if I break it to you now, but don't tell anyone else." She took a deep breath. "I left on Friday when you told me. Booked into a hotel, even though I thought you were crazy."

She paused. "*And?*" I prompted her.

"Somebody attacked the people in the apartments next to mine," she said. "Mr and Mrs Andrews, and Mr Hugon. You never met them, did you?"

"I saw Mrs Andrews once." I licked my lips nervously. "Were they killed?" Debbie nodded. Fresh tears sprung to her eyes. "And drained of blood?" I croaked, dreading the answer.

"Yes."

I looked away, ashamed. I never thought the vampaneze would go after Debbie's neighbours. I'd had only her welfare in mind, not anybody else's. I should have staked out her building, anticipating the worst. Three people were dead because I hadn't.

"When did it happen?" I asked sickly.

"Late Saturday night or early Sunday morning. The bodies were discovered yesterday afternoon, but the police didn't track me down until today. They've kept it quiet, but I think the news is breaking. There were news teams swarming around the building when I passed on my way over here."

"Why did the police want to track you down?" I asked.

She glared at me. "If the people either side of the apartment where *you* lived were killed, and you were nowhere to be found, don't you think the police would look for you too?" she snapped.

"Sorry. Dumb question. I wasn't thinking straight."

Lowering her head, she asked very quietly, "Do you know who did it?"

I hesitated before replying. "Yes and no. I don't know their names, but I know what they are and why they did it."

"You must tell the police," she said.

"It wouldn't help. This is beyond them."

Looking at me through her tears, she said, "I'll be released later this evening. They've taken my statement, but they want to run me through it a few more times. When they release me, I'm coming to put some hard questions to *you*. If I'm not happy with your answers, I'll turn you over to them."

"Thank–" She swivelled sharply and stormed off, joining the police officers and proceeding on to Mr Chivers' office "–you," I finished to myself, then slowly headed back for class. The bell rang, signalling the end of lunch — but to me it sounded like a death knell.

CHAPTER FOURTEEN

THE TIME had come to fill Debbie in on the truth, but Steve and Harkat weren't keen on the idea. "What if she informs the police?" Steve screeched.

"It's dangerous," Harkat warned. "Humans are unpredictable at ... the best of times. You can't know how she'll act or what ... she'll do."

"I don't care," I said stubbornly. "The vampaneze aren't toying with us any longer. They know we know about them. They went to kill Debbie. When they couldn't find her, they slaughtered the people living next door. The stakes have risen. We're in deep now. Debbie has to be told how serious this is."

"And if she betrays us to the police?" Steve asked quietly.

"It's a risk we have to take," I sniffed.

"A risk *you* have to take," Steve said pointedly.

"I thought we were in this together," I sighed. "If I was wrong, leave. I won't stop you."

Steve fidgeted in his chair and traced the cross on his bare left palm with the gloved fingers of his right hand. He did that often, like Mr Crepsley stroking his scar when he was thinking. "There's no need to snap," Steve said sullenly. "I'm with you to the end, like I vowed. But you're making a decision that affects all of us. That isn't right. We should vote on this."

I shook my head. "No votes. I can't sacrifice Debbie, any more than you could let Hooky kill me in the alley. I know I'm putting Debbie before our mission, but I can't help that."

"You feel that strongly about her?" Steve asked.

"Yes."

"Then I won't argue any more. Tell her the truth."

"Thanks." I looked to Harkat for his approval.

The Little Person dropped his gaze. "This is wrong. I can't stop you, so I won't try, but ... I don't approve. The group should *always* come before the ... individual." Pulling his mask — the one he needed to filter out the air, which was poisonous to him — up around his mouth, he turned his back on us and brooded in sullen silence.

Debbie turned up shortly before seven. She'd showered and changed clothes — the police had fetched some of her personal items from her apartment — but still looked terrible. "There's a police officer in the lobby," she said as she entered. "They asked if I wanted a personal guard and I said I did. He thinks I came up here to tutor you. I gave him your name. If you object to that — tough!"

"Nice to see you too," I smiled, holding out my hands to

take her coat. She ignored me and walked into the apartment, stopping short when she caught sight of Steve and Harkat (who was facing away from her).

"You didn't say we'd have company," she said stiffly.

"They have to be here," I replied. "They're part of what I have to tell you."

"Who are they?" she asked.

"This is Steve Leopard." Steve took a quick bow. "And that's Harkat Mulds."

For a moment I didn't think Harkat was going to face her. Then he slowly turned around. "Oh, my lord!" Debbie gasped, shocked by his grey, scarred, unnatural features.

"Guess you don't get many like ... *me* in school," Harkat smiled nervously.

"Is..." Debbie licked her lips. "Is he from that institute you told me about? Where you and Evra Von lived?"

"There is no institute. That was a lie."

She eyed me coldly. "What else have you lied about?"

"Everything, more or less," I grinned guiltily. "But the lies stop here. Tonight I'll tell you the truth. By the end you'll either think I'm crazy or wish I'd never told you, but you have to hear me out — your life depends on it."

"Is it a long story?" she asked.

"One of the longest you'll ever hear," Steve answered with a laugh.

"Then I'd better take a pew," she said. She chose a chair, shrugged off her coat, laid it across her lap, and nodded curtly to let me know I could begin.

I started with the Cirque Du Freak and Madam Octa, and took it from there. I quickly covered my years as Mr Crepsley's assistant and my time in Vampire Mountain. I told her about Harkat and the Lord of the Vampaneze. Then I explained why we'd come here, how fake forms had been submitted to Mahler's, how I'd run into Steve and what role he played in this. I finished with the events of the weekend.

There was a long pause at the end.

"It's insane," Debbie finally said. "You can't be serious."

"He is," Steve chuckled.

"Vampires ... ghosts ... vampaneze... It's ludicrous."

"It's true," I said softly. "I can prove it." I raised my fingers to show her the scars on my fingertips.

"Scars don't prove anything," she sneered.

I walked to the window. "Go to the door and face me," I said. Debbie didn't respond. I could see the doubt in her eyes. "Go on," I said. "I won't hurt you." Holding her coat in front of her, she went to the door and stood opposite me. "Keep your eyes open," I said. "Don't even blink if you can help it."

"What are you going to do?" she asked.

"You'll see — or, rather, you won't."

When she was watching carefully, I tensed the muscles in my legs, then dashed forward, drawing up just in front of her. I moved as quickly as I could, quicker than a human eye could follow. To Debbie it must have seemed that I simply disappeared and reappeared before her. Her eyes shot wide and she leant against the door. Turning, I darted back, again faster than she could follow, stopping by the window.

"Ta-da!" Steve said, clapping dryly.

"How did you do that?" Debbie asked, voice trembling. "You just ... you were there ... then you were here ... then..."

"I can move at tremendously fast speeds. I'm strong, too — I could put a fist through any of these walls and not tear the skin on my knuckles. I can leap higher and further than any human. Hold my breath for longer. Live for centuries." I shrugged. "I'm a half-vampire."

"But it isn't possible! Vampires don't..." Debbie took a few steps towards me, then stopped. She was torn between wanting to disbelieve me and knowing in her heart that I was telling the truth.

"I can spend all night proving it to you," I said. "And you can spend all night pretending there's some other logical explanation. The truth's the truth, Debbie. Accept it or don't — it's your call."

"I don't ... I can't..." She studied my eyes for a long, searching moment. Then she nodded and sank back into her chair. "I believe you," she moaned. "Yesterday I wouldn't have, but I saw photos of the Andrews and Mr Hugon after they'd been killed. I don't think anyone human could have done that."

"You see now why I had to tell you?" I asked. "We don't know why the vampaneze lured us here or why they're playing with us, but their plan is surely to kill us. The attack on your neighbours was only the start of the bloodshed. They won't stop with that. You'll be next if they find you."

"But why?" she asked weakly. "If it's you and this Mr Crepsley they want, why come after me?"

"I don't know. It doesn't make sense. That's what's so frightening."

"What are you doing to stop them?" she asked.

"Tracking them by day. Hopefully we'll find them. If we do, we'll fight. With luck, we'll win."

"You've got to tell the police," she insisted. "And the army. They can—"

"No," I said firmly. "The vampaneze are *our* concern. We'll deal with them."

"How can you say that when it's humans they're killing?" She was angry now. "The police have struggled to find the killers because they don't know anything about them. If you'd told them what they should be looking for, they might have put an end to these creatures months ago."

"It doesn't work that way," I said. "It can't."

"It can!" she snapped. "And it will! I'm going to tell the officer in the lobby about this. We'll see what—"

"How will you convince him?" Steve interrupted.

"I'll..." She drew up short.

"He wouldn't believe you," Steve pressed. "He'd think you were mad. He'd call a doctor and they'd take you away to—" he grinned "—*cure* you."

"I could take Darren with me," she said unconvincingly. "He—"

"—would smile sweetly and ask the kind policeman why his teacher was acting so strangely," Steve chortled.

"You're wrong," Debbie said shakily. "I *could* convince people."

"Then go ahead," Steve smirked. "You know where the door is. Best of luck. Send us a postcard to let us know how you got on."

"I don't like you," Debbie snarled. "You're cocky and arrogant."

"You don't have to like me," Steve retorted. "This isn't a popularity contest. It's a matter of life and death. I've studied the vampaneze and killed six of them. Darren and Harkat have fought and killed them too. We know what we have to do to put a stop to them. Do you honestly think you have the right to stand there and tell us our business? You hadn't even *heard* of the vampaneze until a few hours ago!"

Debbie opened her mouth to argue, then closed it. "You're right," she admitted sullenly. "You've risked your lives for the sake of others, and you know more about this than me. I shouldn't be lecturing you. I guess it's the teacher in me." She managed a very feeble smile.

"Then you trust us to deal with it?" I asked. "You'll find a new apartment, maybe move out of the city for a few weeks, until it's over?"

"I trust you," she said, "but if you think I'm running away, you're deluding yourself. I'm staying to fight."

"What are you talking about?" I frowned.

"I'll help you find and kill the vampaneze."

I stared at her, astonished by the simple way she'd put it, as though we were in search of a lost puppy. "Debbie!" I gasped. "Haven't you been listening? These are creatures that can move at super-fast speeds and flick you into the middle of next week with a snap of a finger. What can you – an ordinary human – hope to accomplish?"

"I can explore the tunnels with you," she said, "provide an extra pair of legs, eyes, ears. With me we can split into pairs and cover twice the ground."

"You couldn't keep up." I protested. "We move too fast."

"Through dark tunnels, with the threat of the vampaneze ever present?" She smiled. "I doubt it."

"OK," I agreed, "you could probably match us for pace, but not endurance. We go all day, hour after hour, without pause. You'd tire and fall behind."

"Steve keeps up," she noted.

"Steve's trained himself to track them. Besides," I added, "Steve doesn't have to report to school every day."

"Neither do I," she said. "I'm on compassionate leave. They don't expect me back until the start of next week at the earliest."

"Debbie ... you ... it's..." I sputtered, then turned appealingly to Steve. "Tell her she's out of her mind," I pleaded.

"Actually, I think it's a good idea," he said.

"*What?*" I roared.

"We could do with another pair of legs down there. If she has the guts for it, I say we give her a go."

"And if we run into the vampaneze?" I challenged him. "Do you see Debbie going face to face with Hooky or his pals?"

"I do, as a matter of fact," he smiled. "From what I've seen, she's got a spine of steel."

"Thank you," Debbie said.

"Don't mention it," he laughed, then grew serious. "I can kit her out with an arrow gun. In a scrape we might be glad of an extra body. At least she'd give the vampaneze another target to worry about."

"I won't stand for it," I growled. "Harkat — tell them."

The Little Person's green eyes were thoughtful. "Tell them what, Darren?"

"That it's madness! Lunacy! Stupidity!"

"Is it?" he asked quietly. "If Debbie was any other person, would you be so ... quick to turn down her offer? The odds are against us. We need allies if we are to triumph."

"But—" I began.

"*You* got her into this," Harkat interrupted. "I told you not to. You ignored me. You can't control people once ... you involve them. She knows the danger and she ... accepts it. What excuse have you to reject her offer ... other than you're fond of her and ... don't want to see her harmed?"

Put like that, there was nothing I could say. "Very well," I sighed. "I don't like this, but if you want to pitch in, I guess we have to let you."

"He's so gallant, isn't he?" Steve observed.

"He certainly knows how to make a girl feel welcome," Debbie grinned, then dropped her coat and leant forward. "Now," she said, "let's quit with the time-wasting and get down to business. I want to know everything there is to know about these monsters. What do they look like? Describe their smell. What sort of tracks do they leave? Where do—"

"Quiet!" I snapped, cutting her short.

She stared at me, offended. "What did I—"

"Hush," I said, quieter this time, laying a finger to my lips. I advanced to the door and pressed my ear against it.

"Trouble?" Harkat asked, stepping up beside me.

"I heard soft footsteps in the hallway a minute ago — but no door has opened."

We retreated, communicating with our eyes. Harkat found his arrow gun, then went to check on the window.

"What's happening?" Debbie asked. I could hear the fast, hard beat of her heart.

"Maybe nothing — maybe an attack."

"Vampaneze?" Steve asked grimly.

"I don't know. It could just be an inquisitive maid. But somebody's out there. Maybe they've been eavesdropping, maybe they haven't. Best not to take chances."

Steve swung his arrow gun around and slid an arrow into it.

"Anyone outside?" I asked Harkat.

"No. I think the way's clear if we have to make a ... break for it."

I drew my sword and tested the blade while considering our next move. If we left now, it would be safer – especially for Debbie – but once you start running, it's hard to stop.

"Up for a scrap?" I asked Steve.

He let out an uneven breath. "I've never fought a vampaneze on its feet," he said. "I've always struck by day, while they were sleeping. I don't know how much use I'd be."

"Harkat?" I asked.

"I think you and I should go see ... what's going on," he said. "Steve and Debbie can wait by the window. If they hear sounds of fighting, they ... should leave."

"How?" I asked. "There's no fire escape and they can't scale walls."

"No problem," Steve said. Reaching inside his jacket, he unwrapped a thin rope from around his waist. "I always come prepared," he winked.

"Will that hold two of you?" Harkat asked.

Steve nodded and tied one end of the rope to a radiator. Going to the window, he swung it open and threw the other end of the rope down. "Over here," he said to Debbie, and she went to him without objecting. He got her to climb on to the window sill and back out over it, holding on to the rope, so she was ready to descend in a hurry. "You two do what you have to," Steve said, covering the door with his arrow gun. "We'll get out if things look bad."

I checked with Harkat, then tiptoed to the door and took hold of the handle. "I'll go first," I said, "and drop low. You come straight after me. If you see anyone who looks like they don't belong — scalp them. We'll stop to ask for their credentials later."

I opened the door and dived into the hall, not bothering with a count. Harkat stepped out after me, arrow gun raised. Nobody to my left. I spun right — no one there either. I paused, ears cocked.

Long, tense moments passed. We didn't move. The silence gnawed at our nerves but we ignored it and concentrated —

when you're fighting vampaneze, a second of distraction is all they need.

Then someone coughed overhead.

Dropping to the floor, I twisted on to my back and brought my sword upright, while Harkat swung his arrow gun up.

The figure clinging to the ceiling dropped before Harkat could fire, knocked him across the hallway, then kicked my sword from my hands. I scrambled after it, then stopped at a familiar chuckle. "Game, set and match to me, I think."

Turning, I was greeted with the sight of a chunky man dressed in purple animal skins, with bare feet and dyed green hair. It was my fellow Vampire Prince — Vancha March!

"*Vancha!*" I gasped, as he grabbed me by the scruff of the neck and helped me to my feet. Harkat had risen by himself and was rubbing the back of his head, where Vancha had struck him.

"Darren," Vancha said. "Harkat." He wagged a finger at us. "You should always check the shadows overhead when scanning for danger. If I'd meant to harm you, the two of you would be dead now."

"When did you get back?" I cried excitedly. "Why did you sneak up on us? Where's Mr Crepsley?"

"Larten's on the roof. We got back about fifteen minutes ago. We heard unfamiliar voices in the room, which is why we moved cautiously. Who's in there with you?"

"Come in and I'll introduce you," I grinned, then led him into the room. I told Steve and Debbie that we were safe, and went to the window to call down a wary, wind-bitten, very welcome Mr Crepsley.

CHAPTER FIFTEEN

MR CREPSLEY was every bit as suspicious of Steve as Steve had predicted. Even after I'd told him about the attack and Steve saving my life, he regarded the human with ill-concealed contempt and remained at a distance. "Blood does not change," he growled. "When I tested Steve Leonard's blood, it was the taste of pure evil. Time cannot have diluted that."

"I'm not evil," Steve growled in return. "*You're* the cruel one, making horrible, unfounded accusations. Do you realize how low an opinion I had of myself after you'd dismissed me as a monster? Your ugly rejection almost drove me to evil!"

"It would not, I think, have been a lengthy drive," Mr Crepsley said smoothly.

"You could have been wrong, Larten," Vancha said. The Prince was lying on the couch, feet propped on the TV set, which he'd dragged closer. His skin wasn't as red as it had been when I last saw him (Vancha was convinced he could

132

train himself to survive sunlight, and often strolled about by day for an hour or so, allowing himself to be badly burnt, building up his body's defences). I guessed he must have spent the past few months walled-up inside Vampire Mountain.

"I was not wrong," Mr Crepsley insisted. "I know the taste of evil."

"I wouldn't bet on that," Vancha said, scratching an armpit. A bug fell out and landed on the floor. He guided it away with his right foot. "Blood's not as easy to divine as certain vampires think. I've found traces of 'evil' blood in several people over the decades, and kept tabs on them. Three went bad, so I killed them. The others led normal lives."

"Not all who are *born* evil *commit* evil," Mr Crepsley said, "but I do not believe in taking chances. I cannot trust him."

"That's stupid," I snapped. "You have to judge people by what they do, not by what you believe they might do. Steve's my friend. I'll vouch for him."

"Me too," Harkat said. "I was cautious at first, but I'm confident now that ... he's on our side. It's not just Darren he saved — he also warned him ... to ring Debbie and tell her to get out. She'd be dead otherwise."

Mr Crepsley shook his head stubbornly. "I say we should test his blood again. Vancha can do it. He will see that I am telling the truth."

"There's no point," Vancha said. "If you say there are traces of evil in his blood, I'm sure there are. But people can overcome their natural defects. I know nothing of this man, but I know Darren and Harkat, and I place more faith in their judgement than in the quality of Steve's blood."

Mr Crepsley muttered something under his breath, but he knew he was outnumbered. "Very well," he said mechanically. "I will speak no more of it. But I will keep a *very* close watch on you," he warned Steve.

"Watch away," Steve sniffed in reply.

To clear the air, I asked Vancha why he'd been absent so long. He said he'd reported to Mika Ver Leth and Paris Skyle and told them about the Vampaneze Lord. He would have left immediately, but he saw how close to death Paris was, and decided to see out the Prince's last few months beside him.

"He died well," Vancha said. "When he knew he was no longer able to play his part, he slipped away in secret. We found his body a few nights later, locked in a death embrace with a bear."

"That's horrible!" Debbie gasped, and everybody in the room smiled at her typical human reaction.

"Trust me," I told her, "there's no worse way for a vampire to die than in a bed, peacefully. Paris had more than eight hundred years under his belt. I doubt he left this world with any complaints."

"Still..." she said, troubled.

"That's the vampire way," Vancha said, leaning across to give her hand a comforting squeeze. "I'll take you aside some night and explain it to you," he added, leaving his hand on hers a few seconds longer than necessary.

If Mr Crepsley was going to keep a close eye on Steve, *I* was going to keep an even closer one on Vancha! I could see that he fancied Debbie. I didn't think she'd be attracted to the ill-mannered, mud-stained, smelly Prince — but I wouldn't leave him alone with her to find out!

"Any news of the Vampaneze Lord or Gannen Harst?" I asked, to distract him.

"No," he said. "I told the Generals that Gannen was my brother and gave them a full description of him, but none had seen him recently."

"What of events here?" Mr Crepsley asked. "Has anybody been murdered, apart from Miss Hemlock's neighbours?"

"Please," Debbie smiled. "Call me Debbie."

"If he won't, I certainly will," Vancha grinned and leant across to pat her hand again. I felt like saying something rude, but constrained myself. Vancha saw me puffing up and winked suggestively.

We told Mr Crepsley and Vancha how quiet things had been before 'Hooky' attacked me in the alley. "I don't like the sound of this Hooky," Vancha grumbled. "I've never heard of a hook-handed vampaneze before. By tradition, a vampaneze would rather do without a lost leg or arm than replace it with an artificial limb. It's strange."

"What is stranger is that he has not attacked since," Mr Crepsley said. "If this vampaneze is in league with those who sent Darren's particulars to Mahler's, he knows the address of this hotel — so why not attack him here?"

"You think there might be two bands of vampaneze at work?" Vancha asked.

"Possibly. Or it could be that the vampaneze are responsible for the murders, while another — perhaps Desmond Tiny — set up Darren at school. Mr Tiny could also have arranged for the hook-handed vampaneze to cross paths with Darren."

"But how did Hooky recognize Darren?" Harkat asked.

"Maybe by the scent of Darren's blood," Mr Crepsley said.

"I don't like this," Vancha grumbled. "Too many 'ifs' and 'buts'. Too twisted by far. I say we get out and leave the humans to fend for themselves."

"I am inclined to agree with you," Mr Crepsley said. "It pains me to say it, but perhaps our purposes would be best served by retreat."

"Then retreat and be damned!" Debbie snapped, and we all stared at her as she got to her feet and faced Mr Crepsley and Vancha, hands bunched into fists, eyes on fire. "What sort of monsters are you?" she snarled. "You talk of people as if we're inferior beings who don't matter!"

"May I remind you, madam," Mr Crepsley replied stiffly, "that we came here to fight the vampaneze and protect you and your kind?"

"Should we be grateful?" she sneered. "You did what anyone with even a trace of humanity would have done. And before you come back with that 'We aren't human' crud, you don't have to be human to be humane!"

"She's a fiery wench, isn't she?" Vancha remarked to me in a stage-whisper. "I could easily fall in love with a woman like this."

"Fall somewhere else," I responded quickly.

Debbie paid no attention to our brief bit of interplay. Her eyes were fixed on Mr Crepsley, who was gazing coolly back at her. "Would you ask us to stay and sacrifice our lives?" he said quietly.

"I'm asking nothing," she retorted. "But if you leave and the killing continues, will you be able to live with yourselves? Can you turn a deaf ear to the cries of those who'll die?"

Mr Crepsley maintained eye contact with Debbie a few beats more, then averted his gaze and muttered softly, "No." Debbie sat, satisfied. "But we cannot chase shadows indefinitely," Mr Crepsley said. "Darren, Vancha and I are on a mission, which has been deferred too long already. We must think about moving on."

He faced Vancha. "I suggest we remain one more week, until the end of next weekend. We will do all in our power to engage the vampaneze, but if they continue to evade us, we should concede defeat and withdraw."

Vancha nodded slowly. "I'd rather get out now, but that's acceptable. Darren?"

"A week," I agreed, then caught Debbie's eye and shrugged. "It's the best we can do," I whispered.

"*I* can do more," Harkat said. "I am not tied to the mission as you ... three are. I will stay beyond the deadline, if matters ... are not resolved by then."

"Me too," Steve said. "I won't quit until the end."

"Thank you," Debbie said softly. "Thank you all." Then she grinned weakly at me and said, "All for one and one for all?"

I grinned back. "All for one and one for all," I agreed, and then everyone in the room repeated it, unbidden, one at a time — although Mr Crepsley did glance at Steve and grunt ironically when it was his turn to make the vow!

CHAPTER SIXTEEN

IT WAS almost dawn before we got to bed (Debbie dismissed her police guard earlier in the night). Everyone crammed into the two hotel rooms. Harkat, Vancha and I slept on the floor, Mr Crepsley in his bed, Steve on the couch, and Debbie in the bed in the other room. Vancha had offered to share Debbie's bed if she wanted someone to keep her warm.

"Thanks," she'd said coyly, "but I'd rather sleep with an orang-utan."

"She likes me!" Vancha declared as she left. "They always play hard to get when they like me!"

At dusk, Mr Crepsley and I checked out of the hotel. Now that Vancha, Steve and Debbie had joined us, we needed to find somewhere quieter. Steve's almost deserted apartment block was ideal. We took over the two apartments next to his and moved straight in. A quick spot of tidying-up and the rooms were ready to inhabit. They weren't comfortable – they were cold and damp – but they'd suffice.

Then it was time to go vampaneze hunting.

We paired off into three teams. I wanted to go with Debbie, but Mr Crepsley said it would be better if she accompanied one of the full-vampires. Vancha immediately offered to be her partner, but I put a quick stop to that idea. In the end we agreed that Debbie would go with Mr Crepsley, Steve with Vancha, and Harkat with me.

Along with our weapons, each of us carried a mobile phone. Vancha didn't like phones – a tom-tom drum was the closest he'd got to modern telecommunications – but we convinced him that it made sense — this way, if one of us found the vampaneze, we'd be able to summon the others swiftly.

Disregarding the tunnels we'd already examined, and those that were used regularly by humans, we divided up the city's underground terrain into three sectors, assigned one per team, and descended into darkness.

A long, disappointing night lay ahead of us. Nobody found any trace of the vampaneze, although Vancha and Steve discovered a human corpse that had been stashed away by the blood-suckers many weeks earlier. They made a note of where it was, and Steve said he'd inform the authorities later, when we'd finished searching, so the body could be claimed and buried.

Debbie looked like a ghost when we met at Steve's apartment the following morning. Her hair was wet and scraggly, her clothes torn, her cheeks scratched, her hands cut by sharp stones and old pipes. While I cleaned out her cuts and bandaged her hands, she stared ahead at the wall, dark rims around her eyes.

"How do you do it, night after night?" she asked in a weak voice.

"We're stronger than humans," I replied. "Fitter and faster. I tried telling you that before, but you wouldn't listen."

"But Steve isn't a vampire."

"He works out. And he's had years of practice." I paused and studied her weary brown eyes. "You don't have to come with us," I said. "You could co-ordinate the search from here. You'd be more use up here than—"

"No," she interrupted firmly. "I said I'd do it and I will."

"OK," I sighed. I finished dressing her wounds and helped her hobble to bed. We'd said nothing about our argument on Friday — this wasn't the time for personal problems.

Mr Crepsley was smiling when I returned. "She will make it," he said.

"You think so?" I asked.

He nodded. "I made no allowances. I held to a steady pace. Yet she kept up and did not complain. It has taken its toll — that is natural — but she will be stronger after a good day's sleep. She will not let us down."

Debbie looked no better when she woke late that evening, but perked up after a hot meal and shower, and was first out the door, nipping down to the shops to buy a strong pair of gloves, water-resistant boots and new clothes. She also tied her hair back and wore a baseball cap, and when we parted that night, I couldn't help admiring how fierce (but beautiful) she looked. I was glad it wasn't *me* she was coming after with the arrow gun she'd borrowed from Steve!

Wednesday was another wash-out, as was Thursday. We knew the vampaneze were down here, but the system of tunnels was vast, and it seemed as if we were never going to find them. Early Friday morning, as Harkat and I were making our way back to base, I stopped at a newspaper stand to buy some papers and catch up with the news. This was the first time since the weekend that I'd paused to check on the state of the world, and as I thumbed through the uppermost paper, a small article caught my eye and I came to a stop.

"What's wrong?" Harkat asked.

I didn't answer. I was too busy reading. The article was about a boy the police were looking for. He was missing, a presumed victim of the killers who'd struck again on Tuesday, murdering a young girl. The wanted boy's name? *Darren Horston!*

I discussed the article with Mr Crepsley and Vancha after Debbie had gone to bed (I didn't want to alarm her). It said simply that I'd been at school on Monday and hadn't been seen since. The police had checked up on me, as they were checking on all students who'd gone absent without contacting their schools (I forgot to phone in to say that I was sick). When they couldn't find me, they'd issued a general description and a plea for anyone who knew anything about me to come forward. They were also 'interested in talking to' my 'father — Vur Horston'.

I suggested ringing Mahler's to say I was OK, but Mr Crepsley thought it would be better if I went in personally. "If you call, they may want to send someone to interview you. And if we ignore the problem, someone might spot you and alert the police."

We agreed I should go in, pretend I'd been sick and that my father moved me to my uncle's house for the good of my health. I'd stay for a few classes — just long enough to assure everyone that I was OK — then say I felt sick again and ask one of my teachers to call my 'uncle' Steve to collect me. He'd remark to the teacher that my father had gone for a job interview, which would be the excuse we'd use on Monday — my father got the job, had to start straightaway, and had sent for me to join him in another city.

It was an unwelcome distraction, but I wanted to be free to throw my weight behind the search for the vampaneze this weekend, so I dressed up in my school uniform and headed in. I reported to Mr Chivers' office twenty minutes before the start of class, thinking I'd have to wait for the perennial late-bird, but was surprised to find him in residence. I knocked and entered at his call. "Darren!" he gasped when he saw me. He jumped up and grasped my shoulders. "Where have you been? What happened? Why didn't you call?"

I ran through my story and apologized for not contacting him. I said I'd only found out that people were looking for me this morning. I also told him I hadn't been keeping up with the news, and that my father was away on business. Mr Chivers scolded me for not letting them know where I was, but was too relieved to find me safe and well to bear me a grudge.

"I'd almost given up on you," he sighed, running a hand through hair that hadn't been washed lately. He looked old and shaken. "Wouldn't it have been awful if you'd been taken as well? Two in a week... It doesn't bear thinking about."

"Two, sir?" I asked.

"Yes. Losing Tara was terrible, but if we'd—"

"Tara?" I interrupted sharply.

"Tara Williams. The girl who was killed last Tuesday." He stared at me incredulously. "Surely you heard."

"I read the name in the papers. Was she a student at Mahler's?"

"Great heavens, boy, don't you know?" he boomed.

"Know what?"

"Tara Williams was a classmate of yours! That's why we were so worried — we thought maybe the two of you had been together when the killer struck."

I ran the name through my memory banks but couldn't match it to a face. I'd met lots of people since coming to Mahler's, but hadn't got to know many, and hardly any of the few I knew were girls.

"You must know her," Mr Chivers insisted. "You sat next to her in English!"

I froze, her face suddenly clicking into place. A small girl, light brown hair, silver braces on her teeth, very quiet. She'd sat to the left of me in English. She let me share her poetry book one day when I left mine in the hotel by accident.

"Oh, no," I moaned, certain this was no coincidence.

"Are you all right?" Mr Chivers asked. "Would you care for something to drink?"

I shook my head numbly. "Tara Williams," I muttered weakly, feeling a chill spread through my body from the inside out. First Debbie's neighbours. Now one of my classmates. Who would be next...?

"Oh, no!" I moaned again, but louder this time. Because I'd just remembered who sat to my right in English — *Richard*!

CHAPTER SEVENTEEN

I ASKED Mr Chivers if I could take the day off. I said I hadn't been feeling well to begin with, and couldn't face classes with the thought of Tara on my mind. He agreed that I'd be better off at home. "Darren," he said as I was leaving, "will you stay in this weekend and take care?"

"Yes, sir," I lied, then hurried downstairs to look for Richard.

Smickey Martin and a couple of his friends were lounging by the entrance as I hit the ground floor. He'd said nothing to me since our run-in on the stairs – he'd shown his true yellow colours by fleeing – but he called out jeeringly when he saw me. "Look what the cat's dragged in! Shame — I thought the vampires had done for you, like they did for Ta-ta Williams." Pausing, I stomped across to face him. He looked wary. "Watch yourself, Horsty," he growled. "If you get in my face, I'll–"

I grabbed the front of his jumper, lifted him off the ground and held him high above my head. He shrieked like a little child and slapped and kicked at me, but I didn't let go, only shook him roughly until he was quiet. "I'm looking for Richard Montrose," I said. "Have you seen him?" Smickey glared at me and said nothing. With my left fingers and thumb, I caught his nose and squeezed until he wailed. "Have you seen him?" I asked again.

"Yuhs!" he squealed.

I let go of his nose. "When? Where?"

"A few minutes ago," he mumbled. "Heading for the computer room."

I sighed, relieved, and gently lowered Smickey. "Thanks," I said. Smickey told me what I could do with my thanks. Smiling, I waved a sarcastic goodbye to the humbled bully, then left the building, satisfied that Richard was safe — at least until night...

At Steve's I woke the sleeping vampires and humans — Harkat was already awake — and discussed the latest twist with them. This was the first Debbie had heard about the murdered girl — she hadn't seen the papers — and the news struck her hard. "Tara," she whispered, tears in her eyes. "What sort of a beast would pick on an innocent young child like Tara?"

I told them about Richard, and put forward the proposal that he was next on the vampaneze hit list. "Not necessarily," Mr Crepsley said. "I think they *will* go after another of your classmates – just as they executed those living to either side of Debbie – but they might go for the boy or girl sitting in front of or behind you."

"But Richard's my friend," I pointed out. "I barely know the others."

"I do not think the vampaneze are aware of that," he said. "If they were, they would have targeted Richard first."

"We need to stake out all three," Vancha said. "Do we know where they live?"

"I can find out," Debbie said, wiping tears from her cheeks. Vancha tossed her a dirty scrap of cloth, which she accepted gratefully. "The student files are accessible by remote computer. I know the password. I'll go to an Internet café, tap into the files and get their addresses."

"What do we do when – *if* – they attack?" Steve asked.

"We do to them what they did to Tara," Debbie growled before any of the rest of us could answer.

"You think that's wise?" Steve responded. "We know there's more than one of them in operation, but I doubt they'll all turn out to kill a child. Wouldn't it be wiser to trace the attacker back to—"

"Hold on," Debbie interrupted. "Are you saying we let them kill Richard or one of the others?"

"It makes sense. Our primary aim is to—"

Debbie slapped his face before he got any further. "Animal!" she hissed.

Steve stared at her emotionlessly. "I am what I have to be," he said. "We won't stop the vampaneze by being civilized."

"You ... you..." She couldn't think of anything dreadful enough to call him.

"He's got a point," Vancha interceded. Debbie turned on him, appalled. "Well, he *has*," Vancha grumbled, dropping his gaze. "I don't like the idea of letting them kill another child, but if it means saving others..."

"No," Debbie said. "No sacrifices. I won't allow it."

"Me neither," I said.

"Have you an alternative suggestion?" Steve asked.

"Injury," Mr Crepsley answered when the rest of us were silent. "We stake out the houses, wait for a vampaneze, then shoot him with an arrow before he strikes. But we do not kill him — we target his legs or arms. Then we follow and, if we are lucky, he will lead us back to his companions."

"I dunno," Vancha muttered. "You, me and Darren can't use those guns — it's not the vampire way — which means we'll have to rely upon the aim of Steve, Harkat and Debbie."

"I won't miss," Steve vowed.

"I won't either," Debbie said.

"Nor me," Harkat added.

"Maybe you won't," Vancha agreed, "but if there are two or more of them, you won't have time to target a second — the arrow guns are single-shooters."

"It is a risk we must take," Mr Crepsley said. "Now, Debbie, you should go to one of these *inferno net* cafés and find the addresses as soon as possible, then get to bed and sleep. We must be ready for action when night comes."

✻   ✻   ✻

Mr Crepsley and Debbie staked out the house of Derek Barry, the boy who sat in front of me in English. Vancha and Steve took responsibility for Gretchen Kelton (Gretch the Wretch, as Smickey Martin called her), who sat behind me. Harkat and I covered the Montrose household.

Friday was a dark, cold, wet night. Richard lived in a big house with his parents and several brothers and sisters. There were lots of upper windows the vampaneze could use to get in. We couldn't cover them all. But vampaneze almost never kill people in their homes — it was how the myth that vampires can't cross a threshold without being invited started — and although Debbie's neighbours had been killed in their apartments, all the others had been attacked in the open.

Nothing happened that night. Richard stayed indoors the whole time. I caught glimpses of him and his family through the curtains every now and then, and envied them their simple lives — none of the Montroses would ever have to stake out a house, anticipating an attack by dark-souled monsters of the night.

When the family was all in bed and the lights went off, Harkat and I took to the roof of the building, where we remained the rest of the night, hidden in the shadows, keeping guard. We left with the rising sun and met the others back at the apartments. They'd had a quiet night too. Nobody had seen any vampaneze.

"The army are back," Vancha noted, referring to the soldiers who'd returned to guard the streets following the murder of Tara Williams. "We'll have to take care not to get in their way — they could mistake us for the killers and open fire."

After Debbie had gone to bed, the rest of us discussed our post-weekend plans. Although Mr Crepsley, Vancha and I had agreed to leave on Monday if we hadn't run down the vampaneze, I thought we should reconsider — things had changed with the murder of Tara and the threat to Richard.

The vampires were having none of it. "A vow's a vow," Vancha insisted. "We set a deadline and must stick to it. If we postpone leaving once, we'll postpone again."

"Vancha is right," Mr Crepsley agreed. "Whether we sight our opponents or not, on Monday we leave. It will not be pleasant, but our quest takes priority. We must do what is best for the clan."

I had to go along with them. Indecision is the source of chaos, as Paris Skyle used to say. This wasn't the time to risk a rift with my two closest allies.

As things worked out, I needn't have worried, because late that Saturday, with heavy clouds masking an almost full moon, the vampaneze finally struck — and all bloody hell broke loose!

CHAPTER EIGHTEEN

HARKAT SAW him first. It was a quarter past eight. Richard and one of his brothers had left the house to go to a nearby shop and were returning with bags full of shopping. We'd shadowed them every step of the way. Richard was laughing at some joke his brother had cracked, when Harkat put a hand on my shoulder and pointed to the skyline. It took me no more than a second to spot the figure crossing the roof of a large apartment store, trailing the boys below.

"Is it Hooky?" Harkat asked.

"I don't know," I said, straining my eyes. "He's not close enough to the edge. I can't see."

The brothers were approaching the mouth of an alley that they had to walk through to get home. That was the logical place for the vampaneze to strike, so Harkat and I hurried after the boys, until we were only a few metres behind when they turned off the main street. We hung back as they started down the alley. Harkat produced his arrow gun (he'd removed the trigger-guard, to accommodate his large finger) and loaded it. I took a couple of throwing knives (courtesy of Vancha) from my belt, ready to back Harkat up if he missed.

Richard and his brother were halfway down the alley when the vampaneze appeared. I saw his gold and silver hooks first – it *was* Hooky! – then his head came into view, masked by a balaclava as it had been before. He would have seen us if he'd checked, but he had eyes only for the humans.

Hooky advanced to the edge of the wall, then skulked along after the brothers, stealthy as a cat. He presented a perfect target, and I was tempted to tell Harkat to shoot to kill. But there were other fish in the vampaneze sea, and if we didn't use this one as bait, we'd never catch them. "His left leg," I whispered. "Below the knee. That'll slow him down."

Harkat nodded without taking his eyes off the vampaneze. I could see Hooky preparing to leap. I wanted to ask Harkat what he was waiting for, but that would have distracted him. Then, as Hooky crouched low to jump, Harkat squeezed the trigger and sent his arrow flying through the darkness. It struck Hooky exactly where I'd suggested. The vampaneze howled with pain and toppled clumsily from the wall. Richard and his brother jumped and dropped their bags. They stared at the person writhing on the floor, not sure whether to flee or go to his aid.

"Get out of here!" I roared, stepping forward, covering my face with my hands so that Richard couldn't identify me.

"Run now if you want to live!" That decided them. Leaving the bags, they bolted. For a couple of humans, it was amazing how fast they could run.

Hooky, meanwhile, was back on his feet. "My leg!" he roared, tugging at the arrow. But Steve was a cunning designer and it wouldn't come loose. Hooky pulled again, harder, and it snapped off in his hand, leaving the head embedded in the muscles of his lower leg. "*Aiiiieeee!*" Hooky screamed, throwing the useless shaft at us.

"Move in," I said to Harkat, deliberately louder than necessary. "We'll trap him and finish him off."

Hooky stiffened when he heard that, the whimpers dying on his lips. Realizing the danger he was in, he tried leaping back up on to the wall. But his left leg was no good and he couldn't manage the jump. Cursing, he pulled a knife out of his belt and propelled it towards us. We had to duck sharply to avoid it, which gave Hooky the time he needed to turn and flee — exactly what we wanted!

As we started after the vampaneze, Harkat phoned the others and told them what was happening. It was his job to keep them informed of developments — I had to focus on Hooky and make sure we didn't lose him.

He'd disappeared from sight when I reached the end of the alley, and for an awful moment I thought he'd escaped. But then I saw drops of blood on the pavement and followed them to the mouth of another alley, where I found him scaling a low wall. I let him get up, and then on to the roof of a neighbouring house, before going after him. It suited my purposes far better to have him up above the streets for the duration of the chase, illuminated by the glow of street lamps, out of the way of police and soldiers.

Hooky was waiting for me on the roof. He'd torn tiles loose and launched them at me, howling like a rabid dog. I dodged one, but had to use my hands to protect myself from the other. It shattered over my knuckles, but caused no real damage. The hook-handed vampaneze advanced, snarling. I was momentarily confused when I noticed that one of his eyes no longer glowed red — it was an ordinary blue or green colour — but I'd no time to mull it over. Bringing my knives up, I prepared to meet the killer's challenge. I didn't want to kill him before he'd had a chance to lead us back to his companions, but if I had to, I would.

Before he could test me, Vancha and Steve appeared. Steve fired an arrow at the vampaneze — missing on purpose — and Vancha leapt on to the wall. Hooky howled again, sent another few tiles flying towards us, then scrambled up the roof and down the other side.

"Are you OK?" Vancha asked, stopping beside me.

"Yes. We got him in the leg. He's bleeding."

"I noticed."

There was a small pool of blood nearby. I dipped a finger into it and sniffed. It smelt of vampaneze blood, but I still asked Vancha to test it. "It's vampaneze," he said, tasting it. "Why wouldn't it be?" I explained about Hooky's eyes. "Strange," he grunted, but said no more. Helping me to my feet, he scuttled to the top of the roof, checked to make sure

Hooky wasn't lying in wait for us, then beckoned me to follow. The chase was on!

While Vancha and I trailed the vampaneze across the rooftops, Harkat and Steve kept abreast of us on the ground, slowing only to negotiate their way around roadblocks or police patrols. About five minutes into the chase, Mr Crepsley and Debbie connected with us, Debbie joining those below, the vampire taking to the roofs.

We could have closed in on Hooky – he was having a hard time, slowed by his injured leg, the pain and loss of blood – but we allowed him to remain ahead of us. There was no way he could ditch us up here. If we'd wanted to kill him, it would have been a simple matter to reel him in. But we didn't want to kill him — yet!

"We mustn't let him grow suspicious," Vancha said after several minutes of silence. "If we hang back too long, he'll guess something's up. Time to drive him to earth." Vancha moved ahead of us, until he was within shuriken-throwing range of the vampaneze. He took a throwing star from the belts looped around his chest, aimed carefully and sent it skimming off a chimney just above Hooky's head.

Whirling, the vampaneze shouted something unintelligible back at us and angrily shook a golden hook. Vancha silenced him with another shuriken, which flew even closer to its mark than the first. Dropping to his belly, Hooky slid to the edge of the roof, where he grabbed on to the guttering with his hooks, halting his fall. He hung over open space a moment, checked the area underneath, jerked his hooks clear of the guttering and then dropped. It was a four-storey fall, but that was nothing to a vampaneze.

"Here we go," Mr Crepsley muttered, making for a nearby fire escape. "Call the others and warn them — we do not want them running into him on the streets."

I did that while jogging down the steps of the fire escape. They were a block and a half behind us. I told them to hold position until further notice. While Mr Crepsley and I followed the vampaneze on the ground, Vancha kept sight of him from the rooftops, making sure he couldn't take to the roofs again, narrowing his options so that he had to choose between the streets and the tunnels.

After three minutes of frenzied running, he chose the tunnels.

We found a discarded manhole cover and a trail of blood leading down into the darkness. "This is it," I sighed nervously as we stood waiting for Vancha. I hit the redial button on my mobile and summoned the others. When they arrived, we paired off into our regular teams, and climbed down into the tunnels. Each of us knew what we had to do and no words were exchanged.

Vancha and Steve led the pursuit. The rest of us trailed behind, covering adjacent tunnels, so Hooky couldn't double back. It wasn't easy tracking Hooky down here. The water in the tunnels had washed much of his blood away, and the darkness made it hard to see very far ahead. But we'd become accustomed to these tight, dark spaces, and we moved quickly and efficiently, keeping close, picking up on the slightest identifying marks.

Hooky led us deeper into the tunnels than we'd ever been. Even the mad vampaneze, Murlough, hadn't delved this deeply into the underbelly of the city. Was Hooky heading for his companions and help, or simply trying to lose us?

"We must be nearing the city limits," Harkat remarked as we rested a moment. "The tunnels must run out soon, or else..."

"What?" I asked when he didn't continue.

"They could open up," he said. "Perhaps he is making a break ... for freedom. If he reaches open countryside and ... has a clear run, he can flit to safety."

"Won't his wounds stop him doing that?" I asked.

"Perhaps. But if he is desperate enough ... perhaps not."

We resumed the chase and caught up with Vancha and Steve. Harkat told Vancha what he thought Hooky was planning. Vancha replied that he'd already thought of that, and was gradually closing in on the fleeing vampaneze — if Hooky angled for the surface, Vancha would head him off and make an end of him.

But, to our surprise, instead of heading upwards, the vampaneze led us ever further down. I'd no idea the tunnels ran this deep, and couldn't imagine what they were for — they were modern in design, and showed no signs of having been used. As I was pondering it, Vancha came to a standstill and I almost walked into him.

"What is it?" I asked.

"He's stopped," Vancha whispered. "There's a room or cave up ahead and he's come to a halt."

"Waiting for us, to make a final stand?" I suggested.

"Perhaps," Vancha replied uneasily. "He's lost a lot of blood and the pace of the chase must be sapping his energy. But why stop now? Why here?" He shook his head. "I don't like it."

As Mr Crepsley and Debbie arrived, Steve unstrapped his arrow gun and loaded it by torchlight.

"Careful!" I hissed. "He'll see the light."

Steve shrugged. "So? He knows we're here. We might as well operate by light as in darkness."

That made sense, so we all lit the torches we'd brought, keeping the lights dim so as not to create too many distracting shadows.

"Do we go after him," Steve asked, "or stay here and wait for him to attack?"

"We go in," Mr Crepsley answered after the briefest of pauses.

"Aye," Vancha said. "In."

I studied Debbie. She was trembling and looked ready to collapse. "You can wait out here if you like," I told her.

"No," she said. "I'm coming." She stopped trembling. "For Tara."

"Steve and Debbie will keep to the back," Vancha said, loosening a few of his shurikens. "Larten and I will lead. Darren and Harkat in the middle." Everybody nodded obediently. "If he's alone, I'll take him," Vancha went on. "An even fight, one-on-one. If he has *company*—" he grinned humourlessly "—it's everyone for themselves."

One final check to make sure we were ready and he advanced, Mr Crepsley to his right, Harkat and I close behind, Steve and Debbie bringing up the rear.

We found ourselves in a large, domed room, modern like the tunnels. A handful of candles jutted from the walls, casting a gloomy, flickering light. There was another way into the room directly across from us, but it was barred by a heavy, round, metal door, like those used for walk-in safes in banks. Hooky had squatted a few metres in front of the door. His knees were drawn up to cover his face, and his hands were busy trying to pry the arrow head from his leg.

We fanned out, Vancha in front, the rest of us forming a protective semi-circle behind him. "The game's over," Vancha said, holding back, examining the shadows for traces of other vampaneze.

"Think so?" Hooky snorted and looked up at us with his one red eye and one blue-green. "*I* think it's only beginning." The vampaneze clashed his hooks together. Once. Twice. Three times.

And someone dropped from the ceiling.

The someone landed beside Hooky. Stood and faced us. His face was purple and his eyes were blood-red — a vampaneze. Someone else dropped. Another. More. I felt sick inside as I watched vampaneze drop. There were human vampets among them too, dressed in brown shirts and black trousers, with skinned heads, a tattooed 'V' above either ear, and red circles painted around their eyes, carrying rifles, pistols and crossbows.

I counted nine vampaneze and fourteen vampets, not including Hooky. We'd walked into a trap, and as I stared around at the armed, grim-faced warriors, I knew we'd need all the luck of the vampires just to scrape out of this alive.

CHAPTER NINETEEN

AS POOR as the odds were, they were about to get even worse. As we stood awaiting the onslaught, the huge door behind Hooky opened and four more vampaneze stepped through to join the others. That made it twenty-eight to six. We hadn't a hope.

"Not so pleased with yourselves now, are you?" Hooky jeered, hobbling forward a few gleeful paces.

"I don't know about that," Vancha sniffed. "This just means more of you for us to kill."

Hooky's smile vanished. "Are you arrogant or ignorant?" he snapped.

"Neither," Vancha said, gazing calmly at our foes. "I'm a vampire."

"You really think you stand a chance against us?" Hooky sneered.

"Yes," Vancha answered softly. "Were we fighting honest, noble vampaneze, I'd think otherwise. But a vampaneze who sends armed humans to fight his battles is a coward, without honour. I have nothing to fear from such pitiable beasts."

"Be careful what you say," the vampaneze to the left of Hooky growled. "We don't take kindly to insults."

"*We're* the ones who've been insulted," Vancha replied. "There's honour in dying at the hands of a worthy foe. If you'd sent your best warriors against us and killed us, we'd have died with smiles on our lips. But to send these ... these..." He spat into the dust of the floor. "There's no word low enough to describe them."

The vampets bristled at that, but the vampaneze looked uneasy, almost ashamed, and I realized they were no fonder of the vampets than we were. Vancha noticed this too and slowly loosened his belts of shurikens. "Drop your arrow guns," he said to Steve, Harkat and Debbie. They stared at him dumbly. "Do it!" he insisted gruffly and they complied. Vancha held up his bare hands. "We've put our long-range weapons aside. Will you order your pets to do the same and engage us honourably — or will you have us shot down in cold blood like the curs I think you are?"

"Shoot them!" Hooky screamed, his voice laced with hatred. "Shoot them all!"

The vampets raised their weapons and took aim.

"No!" the vampaneze to Hooky's left bellowed and the vampets paused. "By all the shadows of the night, I say no!"

Hooky whirled on him. "Are you crazy?"

"Beware," the vampaneze warned him. "If you cross me on this, I'll kill you where you stand."

Hooky stepped back, stunned. The vampaneze faced the vampets. "Drop your guns," he commanded. "We'll fight with our traditional weapons. With *honour*."

The vampets obeyed the order. Vancha turned and winked at us while they were laying their weapons aside. Then he faced the vampaneze again. "Before we start," he said, "I'd like to know what manner of creature this thing with the hooks is."

"I'm a vampaneze!" Hooky replied indignantly.

"Really?" Vancha smirked. "I've never seen one with mismatched eyes before."

Hooky's eyes twitched exploratively. "Damn!" he shouted. "It must have slipped out when I fell."

"What slipped out?" Vancha asked.

"A contact lens," I answered softly. "He's wearing red contact lenses."

"No I'm not!" Hooky yelled. "That's a lie! Tell them, Bargen. My eyes are as red as yours and my skin's as purple."

The vampaneze to Hooky's left shuffled his feet with embarrassment. "He *is* a vampaneze," he said, "but he's only been recently blooded. He wanted to look like the rest of us, so he wears contacts and..." Bargen coughed into a fist. "He paints his face and body purple."

"Traitor!" Hooky howled.

Bargen looked up at him, disgusted, then spat into the dust of the floor as Vancha had moments before.

"What has the world come to when the vampaneze blood maniacs like this and recruit humans to fight for them?"

Vancha asked quietly and there was no mockery in his voice — it was a genuine, puzzled query.

"Times change," Bargen answered. "We don't like the changes, but we accept them. Our Lord has said it must be so."

"This is what the great Lord of the Vampaneze has brought to his people?" Vancha barked. "Human thugs and crazy, hook-handed monsters?"

"I'm not crazy!" Hooky shouted. "Except crazy with rage!" He pointed at me and snarled. "And it's all *his* fault."

Vancha turned and stared at me, as did everybody else in the room.

"Darren?" Mr Crepsley asked quietly.

"I don't know what he's talking about," I said.

"Liar!" Hooky laughed and started dancing. "Liar, liar, pants on fire!"

"Do you know this *creature*?" Mr Crepsley enquired.

"No," I insisted. "The first time I saw him was when he attacked me in the alley. I never—"

"Lies!" Hooky screamed, then stopped dancing and glared at me. "Pretend all you like, man, but you know who I am. And you know what you did to drive me to this." He held up his arms, so the hooks glinted in the light of the candles.

"Honestly," I swore, "I haven't a clue what you're on about."

"No?" he sneered. "It's easy to lie to a mask. Let's see if you can stick to your lie when faced with—" he removed the balaclava with one quick sweep of his left hooks, revealing his face "—*this!*"

It was a round, heavy, bearded face, smeared with purple paint. For a few seconds I couldn't place it. Then, putting it together with the missing hands, and the familiarity of the voice that I'd previously noted, I nailed him. "*Reggie Veggie?*" I gasped.

"Don't call me that!" he shrieked. "It's *R.V.* — and it stands for Righteous Vampaneze!"

I didn't know whether to laugh or cry. R.V. was a man I'd run into not long after joining the Cirque Du Freak, an eco-warrior who'd devoted his life to the protection of the countryside. We'd been friends until he found me killing animals to feed the Little People. He set out to free the Wolf Man — he thought we were mistreating him — but the savage beast bit his arms off. The last time I'd seen him, he'd been fleeing into the night, screaming loudly, "My hands! My hands!"

Now he was here. With the vampaneze. And I began to understand why I'd been set up and who was behind it. "*You* sent those forms to Mahler's!" I accused him.

He grinned slyly, then shook his head. "With hands like these?" He waved the hooks at me. "They're good for chopping and slicing and gutting, but not for writing. I played my part to get you down here, but it was one with a lot more cunning than me who dreamt the plan up."

"I don't understand," Vancha interrupted. "Who is this lunatic?"

"It's a long story," I said. "I'll tell you later."

"Optimistic to the last," Vancha chuckled.

I stepped closer to R.V., ignoring the threat of the vampaneze and vampets, until I was only a metre or so away. I studied his face silently. He fidgeted but didn't back off. "What happened to you?" I asked, appalled. "You loved life. You were gentle and kind. You were a vegetarian!"

"Not any more," R.V. chuckled. "I eat plenty of meat now and I like it *bloody!*" His smile faded. "*You* happened to me, you and your band of freaks. You ruined my life, man. I wandered the world, alone, frightened, defenceless, until the vampaneze took me in. They gave me strength. They equipped me with new hands. In turn, I helped give them *you.*"

I shook my head sadly. "You're wrong. They haven't made you strong. They've turned you into an abomination."

His face darkened. "Take that back! Take that back or I'll—"

"Before this goes any further," Vancha interrupted dryly, "could I ask one more question? It's my final one." R.V. stared at him in silence. "If *you* didn't set us up, who did?" R.V. said nothing. Nor did the other vampaneze. "Come on!" Vancha shouted. "Don't be shy. Who's the clever boy?"

The silence held a few moments more. Then, from behind us, somebody said in a soft, wicked voice, "*I* am."

I whirled around to see who'd spoken. So did Vancha, Harkat and Mr Crepsley. But Debbie didn't whirl, because she was standing still, a knife pressed to the soft flesh of her throat. And Steve Leopard didn't whirl either, because he was standing beside her — *holding the knife!*

We gawped wordlessly at the pair. I blinked twice, slowly,

thinking maybe that would restore sanity to the world. But it didn't. Steve was still there, holding his knife on Debbie, grinning darkly.

"Take off your gloves," Mr Crepsley said, his voice strained. "Take them off and show us your hands."

Steve smiled knowingly, then put the fingertips of his left hand — which was wrapped around Debbie's throat — to his mouth, gripped the ends of the glove with his teeth, and pulled his hand free. The first thing my eyes went to was the cross carved into the flesh of his palm, the cross he'd made the night he vowed to track me down and kill me. Then my eyes slid from his palm to the end of his fingers, and I understood why Mr Crepsley had asked him to remove the glove.

There were five small scars running along his fingertips — the sign that he was a creature of the night. But Steve hadn't been blooded by a vampire. He'd been blooded by one of the others. *He was a half-vampaneze!*

CHAPTER TWENTY

As THE initial shock faded, a cold, dark hatred grew in the pit of my stomach. I forgot about the vampaneze and vampets and focused entirely on Steve. My best friend. The boy whose life I'd saved. The man I'd welcomed back with open arms. I'd vouched for him. Trusted him. Included him in our plans.

And all along he'd been plotting against us.

I would have gone for him there and then, and ripped him to pieces, except he was using Debbie as a shield. Fast as I was, I wouldn't be able to stop him slashing the knife across her throat. If I attacked, Debbie would die.

"I knew we could not trust him," Mr Crepsley said, looking only slightly less wrathful than I felt. "Blood does not change. I should have killed him years ago."

"Don't be a sore loser," Steve laughed, pulling Debbie even tighter in to him.

"It was all a ploy, wasn't it?" Vancha noted. "The hooked one's attack and your rescue of Darren was staged."

"Of course," Steve smirked. "I knew where they were all along. *I* suckered them in, sending R.V. to this city to spread panic among the humans, knowing it would draw Creepy Crepsley back."

"How did you know?" Mr Crepsley asked, astonished.

"Research," Steve said. "I found out all I could about you. I made you my life's work. It wasn't easy, but I traced you in the end. Found your birth certificate. Connected you to this place. I teamed up with my good friends, the vampaneze, during the course of my travels. They didn't reject me like you did. Through them I learnt that one of their brethren — poor, deranged Murlough — had gone missing here some years ago. Knowing what I did about you and your movements, it wasn't difficult to join the dots.

"What *did* happen with Murlough?" Steve asked. "Did you kill him or merely scare him off?"

Mr Crepsley didn't answer. Nor did I.

"No matter," Steve said. "It's not important. But I figured that if you came back to help these people once, you'd do it again."

"Very clever," Mr Crepsley snarled. His fingers were twitching like spider legs by his sides, and I knew he was itching to wrap them around Steve's throat.

"What I don't understand," Vancha remarked, "is what this lot are doing here." He nodded at Bargen and the other vampaneze and vampets. "Surely they're not here to assist you in your insane quest for revenge."

"Of course not," Steve said. "I'm just a humble half-vampaneze. It's not for me to command my betters. I told them about Murlough, which interested them, but they're here for other reasons, on someone else's say-so."

"Whose?" Vancha asked.

"That would be telling. And we aren't here to tell — we're here to kill!"

Behind us, the vampaneze and vampets advanced. Vancha, Mr Crepsley and Harkat spun to face their challenge. I didn't. I couldn't tear my eyes away from Steve and Debbie. She was weeping, but holding herself steady, looking appealingly in my direction.

"*Why?*" I croaked.

"Why what?" Steve replied.

"Why do you hate us? We did nothing to hurt you."

"*He* said I was evil!" Steve howled, nodding at Mr Crepsley, who didn't turn to remonstrate with him. "And *you* chose his side over mine. You set that spider on me and tried to kill me."

"No! I saved you. I gave up everything so that you could live."

"Nonsense," he snorted. "I know what really happened. You plotted with him against me, so you could take my rightful place among the vampires. You were jealous of me."

"No, Steve," I groaned. "That's madness. You don't know what—"

"Save it!" Steve interrupted. "I'm not interested. Besides, here comes the guest of honour — a man I'm sure you're all just *dying* to meet."

I didn't want to turn away from Steve, but I had to see what he was talking about. Looking over my shoulder, I saw two vague shapes behind the massed vampaneze and vampets. Vancha, Mr Crepsley and Harkat were ignoring Steve's jibes and the pair at the back, concentrating instead on the foes directly in front of them, warding off their early testing jabs. Then the vampaneze parted slightly and I had a clear view of the two behind them.

"Vancha!" I shouted.

"What?" he snapped.

"At the rear — it's..." I licked my lips. The taller of the pair had spotted me and was gazing at me with a neutral, inquisitive expression. The other was dressed in dark green robes, his face covered by a hood.

"Who?" Vancha shouted, knocking aside a vampet's blade with his bare hands.

"It's your brother, Gannen Harst," I said quietly and Vancha stopped fighting. So did Mr Crepsley and Harkat. And so, puzzled, did the vampaneze.

Vancha stood to his fullest height and stared over the heads of those in front of him. Gannen Harst's eyes left mine and locked on Vancha's. The brothers stared at each other. Then Vancha's gaze switched to the person in the robes and hood — the Lord of the Vampaneze!

"*Him! Here!*" Vancha gasped.

"You've met before, I take it," Steve commented snidely.

Vancha ignored the half-vampaneze. "*Here!*" he gasped again, eyes pinned on the leader of the vampaneze, the man we'd sworn to kill. Then he did the last thing the vampaneze had been expecting — with a roar of pure adrenaline, he *charged!*

It was lunacy, one unarmed vampire taking on twenty-eight armed and able opponents, but that lunacy worked in his favour. Before the vampaneze and vampets had time to come to terms with the craziness of Vancha's charge, he'd barrelled through nine or ten of them, knocking them to the ground or into the way of others, and was almost upon Gannen Harst and the Vampaneze Lord before they knew what was happening.

Seizing the moment, Mr Crepsley reacted quicker than anyone else and darted after Vancha. He dived among the vampaneze and vampets, knives outstretched in his extended hands like a pair of talons at the end of a bat's wings, and three of our foes fell, throats or chests slit open.

As Harkat swung in behind the vampires, burying the head of his axe in the skull of a vampet, the last in the line of vampaneze closed ranks on Vancha and blocked his path to their Lord. The Prince lashed at them with his blade-like hands, but they knew what they were doing now, and although he killed one of them, the others surged forward and forced him to a halt.

I should have gone after my companions — killing the Vampaneze Lord meant more than anything else — but my senses were screaming one name only, and it was a name I reacted to impulsively: "*Debbie!*" Swivelling away from the battle, praying that Steve had been distracted by the sudden outbreak, I sent a knife flying towards him. It wasn't intended to hit – I couldn't risk striking Debbie – just to make him duck.

It worked. Startled by the swiftness of my move, Steve jerked his head behind Debbie's for protection. His left arm loosened around her throat, and his right hand – holding the knife – dropped a fraction. As I raced forward, I knew the momentary swing of fortune wasn't enough — he'd still have time to recover and kill Debbie before I reached him. But then Debbie, acting like a trained warrior, dug her left elbow sharply back into Steve's ribs, and broke free of his hold, throwing herself to the floor.

Before Steve could dive after her, I was on him. I grabbed him around the waist and propelled him backwards into the wall. He connected harshly and cried out. Stepping away from him, I sent my right fist smashing into the side of his face. The force of the blow knocked him down. It also nearly broke a couple of small bones in my fingers, but that didn't bother me. Falling upon him, I grabbed his ears, pulled his head up, then smashed it down on the hard concrete floor. He grunted and the lights went out in his eyes. He was dazed and defenceless — mine for the taking.

My hand went for the hilt of my sword. Then I saw Steve's own knife lying close beside his head, and decided it would be more fitting to kill him with that. Picking it up, I positioned it above his dark, monstrous heart and prodded through the material of his shirt to make sure he wasn't protected by a breastplate or some other such armour. Then I raised the knife high above my head and brought it down slowly, determined to strike the mark and put an end to the life of the man I'd once counted as my dearest friend.

CHAPTER TWENTY-ONE

"Stop!" R.V. screamed as my blade descended, and something in his voice made me pause and look back. My heart sank — he had Debbie! He was holding her as Steve had, the hooks of his golden right hand pressed up into the flesh of her jaw. A couple of hooks had lightly punctured the skin and thin streams of blood trickled down the golden blades. "Drop the knife or I slit her like a pig!" R.V. hissed.

If I dropped the knife, Debbie would die anyway, along with the rest of us. There was only one thing for it — I had to try and force a stand-off. Grabbing Steve by his long grey hair, I jammed my knife against the flesh of his throat. "If she dies, he dies," I growled and I saw doubt fill R.V.'s eyes.

"Don't play games with me," the hook-handed vampaneze warned. "Let him go or I kill her."

"If she dies, he dies," I said again.

R.V. cursed, then glanced over his shoulder for help. The

battle was going the way of the vampaneze. Those who'd stumbled in the first few seconds of the fight had regained their feet, and now encircled Vancha, Mr Crepsley and Harkat, who fought back to back, protecting each other, unable to advance or retreat. Beyond the crush, Gannen Harst and the Lord of the Vampaneze looked on.

"Forget about them," I said. "This is between you and me. It's got nothing to do with anybody else." I managed a weak smile. "Or are you afraid to face me on your own?"

R.V. sneered. "I'm afraid of nothing, man. Except..." He stopped.

Guessing what he'd been about to say, I put my head back and howled like a wolf. R.V.'s eyes widened with fear at the sound, but then he collected himself and stood firm. "Howling won't save your tasty little girlfriend," he taunted me.

I had a strange sense of *déjà vu* — Murlough used to speak that way about Debbie, and for a moment it was as though the spirit of the dead vampaneze was alive inside R.V. Then I put such macabre thoughts behind me and concentrated.

"Let's stop wasting each other's time," I said. "You put Debbie aside, I'll put Steve aside, and we'll settle this man to man, winner takes all."

R.V. grinned and shook his head. "No deal. I don't have to risk my neck. I'm holding all the cards."

Keeping Debbie in front of him, he edged towards the exit at the opposite side of the room, skirting the vampaneze.

"What are you doing?" I shouted, moving to block him.

"Stay back!" he roared, digging his hooks deeper into Debbie's jaw, causing her to gasp with pain.

I stopped uncertainly. "Let her go," I said quietly, desperately.

"No," he replied. "I'm taking her. If you try to stop me, I'll kill her."

"I'll kill Steve if you do."

He laughed. "I don't care for Steve as much as you care for precious little Debbie. I'll sacrifice my friend if you'll sacrifice yours. How about it, Shan?" I studied Debbie's round, terrified eyes, then took a step back, clearing the way for R.V. to pass. "Wise move," he grunted, easing past, not turning his back on me.

"If you harm her..." I sobbed.

"I won't," he said. "Not for the time being. I want to see you squirm before I do. But if you kill Steve or come after me..." His cold, mismatched eyes told me what would happen.

Laughing, the hook-handed monster slipped past the vampaneze, then past Gannen Harst and his Lord, vanishing into the gloomy darkness of the tunnel beyond, taking Debbie with him, leaving me and the others to the mercy of the vampaneze.

Now that Debbie was beyond saving, my choices were clear. I could try to help my friends, who were trapped by the vampaneze, or go after the Vampaneze Lord. It took me no time to choose. I couldn't rescue my friends — there were just too many vampaneze and vampets — and even if I could, I wouldn't have — the Vampaneze Lord came first. I'd momentarily forgotten that when Steve seized Debbie, but now my training reasserted itself. Across the way, Steve was still unconscious. No time to finish him off — I'd do it later, if possible. Sneaking around the vampaneze, drawing my sword, meaning to take on Gannen Harst and the figure he guarded.

Harst spotted me, put his fingers to his mouth and whistled loudly. Four of the vampaneze at the rear of the group looked to him, then followed the direction of his finger as he pointed towards me. Turning away from the ruckus, they blocked my path, then advanced.

I might have tried to fight my way through them, hopeless as it was, but then I saw Gannen Harst call another two vampaneze away from the fighting. He gave the Vampaneze Lord to them and they exited down the tunnel that R.V. had fled through. Gannen Harst swung the huge door shut after them and spun a large, circular lock at the centre of it. Without the combination, it would be impossible to get through a door as thick as that.

Gannen Harst stepped up behind the four vampaneze who were converging on me. He clicked his tongue against the roof of his mouth and the vampaneze came to a standstill. Harst looked into my eyes, then made the death's touch sign by pressing his middle finger to the centre of his forehead, the two adjacent fingers over his eyes, and spreading his thumb and little finger out wide. "Even in death, may you be triumphant," he said.

I glanced around swiftly, taking in the state of play. Close to my right, the battle still raged. Mr Crepsley, Vancha and Harkat were cut in many places, bleeding liberally, yet none had sustained fatal wounds. They were on their feet, weapons in hand — except Vancha, whose weapons *were* his hands — keeping the circle of vampaneze and vampets at bay.

I couldn't understand it. Given our foes' superior numbers, they should have overwhelmed and dispatched the trio by now. The longer the fighting progressed, the more damage we were inflicting — at least six vampets and three vampaneze were dead, and several more nursed life-threatening injuries. Yet still they fought warily, judging their blows with care, almost as though they didn't want to kill us.

I reached a snap decision and knew what I had to do. I faced Gannen Harst and screamed, "I'll be triumphant in life!" in defiance, then whipped out a knife and launched it at the vampaneze, throwing it deliberately high. As the five vampaneze ahead of me ducked to avoid the knife, I swivelled and swung with my sword at the vampaneze and vampets packed tightly around Mr Crepsley, Vancha and Harkat. Now that the Lord of the Vampaneze was beyond reach, I was free to help or perish with my friends. A few moments earlier, we'd surely have perished, but the pendulum had swung round slightly in our favour. The pack had been whittled down by half a dozen members — two had left with their Lord, and four more were standing with Gannen Harst. The remaining vampaneze and vampets had spread themselves out to cover for their missing clansmen.

My sword connected with the vampaneze to my right, and narrowly missed the throat of a vampet to my left. The vampaneze and vampet both stepped aside at the same moment, instinctively, in opposite directions, creating a gap. "To me!" I cried at the trio trapped in the middle of the mayhem.

Before the gap could be filled, Harkat burst through, chopping with his axe. More vampaneze and vampets drew back, and Mr Crepsley and Vancha hurried after Harkat, fanning out around him, turning so that they were all facing the same way, instead of having to fight back to back.

We retreated swiftly towards the tunnel leading out of the cavern.

"Quick — block the exit!" one of the four vampaneze with Gannen Harst yelled, moving forward to bar our way.

"Hold," Gannen Harst responded quietly and the vampaneze stopped. He looked back at Harst, puzzled, but Harst only shook his head grimly.

I wasn't sure why Harst had prevented his men from blocking our one route of escape, but I didn't stop to ponder it. As we backed up towards the exit, lashing out at the vampaneze and vampets who pushed forward after us, we passed Steve. He was regaining his senses and was half sitting up. I paused as we came abreast of him, grabbed him by his hair and hauled him to his feet. He yelped and struggled, but then I stuck the edge of my sword to his throat and he went quiet. "You're coming with us!" I hissed in his ear. "If we die, so do you." I'd have killed him then and there, except I remembered what R.V. had said — if I killed Steve, he'd kill Debbie.

As we came to the mouth of the tunnel, a vampet swung a short length of chain at Vancha. The vampire grabbed the chain, yanked the vampet in, caught him by the head, and made to twist it sharply to the right, meaning to snap his neck and kill him.

"Enough!" Gannen Harst bellowed and the vampaneze and vampets closing upon us instantly stopped fighting and dropped back two paces.

Vancha relaxed his lock, but didn't release the vampet, and glared around suspiciously. "What now?" he muttered.

"I do not know," Mr Crepsley said, wiping sweat and blood from his brow. "But they fight most bizarrely. Nothing they do would surprise me."

Gannen Harst pushed through the vampaneze until he was standing in front of his brother. The two didn't look alike – where Vancha was burly, gruff and rough, Gannen was slim, cultured and smooth – but there was a certain way they had of standing and inclining their heads that was very similar.

"Vancha," Gannen greeted his estranged brother.

"Gannen," Vancha replied, not letting go of the vampet, watching the other vampaneze like a hawk in case they made any sudden moves.

Gannen looked at Mr Crepsley, Harkat and me. "We meet again," he said, "as was destined. Last time, you had the beating of me. Now the tables have turned." He paused and gazed around the room at the silent vampaneze and vampets, then at their dead and dying colleagues. Then he glanced at the tunnel behind us. "We could kill you here, in this tunnel, but you would take many of us with you," he sighed. "I tire of needless bloodshed. Shall we strike a deal?"

"What sort of a deal?" Vancha grunted, trying to hide his bewilderment.

"It would be easier for us to slaughter you in the larger tunnels beyond this one. We could pick you off, in our own time, possibly without losing more of our men."

"You want us to make your job easier for you?" Vancha laughed.

"Let me finish," Gannen continued. "As things stand, you have no hope of making it back to the surface alive. If we attack you here, our losses will be great, but all four of you will certainly die. If, on the other hand, we were to give you a head start..." He trailed off into silence, then spoke again. "Fifteen minutes, Vancha. Leave your hostages — you can move more quickly without them — and flee. For fifteen minutes, nobody will follow. You have my word."

"This is a trick," Vancha snarled. "You wouldn't let us go, not like this."

"I don't lie," Gannen said stiffly. "The odds are still in our favour — we know these tunnels better than you do, and will probably catch you before you make it to freedom. But this way you have hope — and I won't have to bury any more of my friends."

Vancha exchanged a furtive glance with Mr Crepsley.

"What about Debbie?" I shouted before either vampire could speak. "I want to take her too!"

Gannen Harst shook his head. "I command those in this room," he said, "but not he of the hooks. She is his now."

"Not good enough," I snorted. "If Debbie doesn't leave, I don't either. I'll stay here and kill as many of you as I can."

"Darren—" Vancha began to protest.

"Do not argue," Mr Crepsley intervened. "I know Darren — your words would be wasted. He will not leave without her. And if he will not leave, nor will I."

Vancha cursed, then looked his brother clean in the eye. "There you have it. If they won't go, I won't either."

Harkat cleared his throat. "These fools don't speak ... for me. *I'll* go." Then he smiled to show he was joking.

Gannen spat between his feet, disgusted. In my arms, Steve stirred and groaned. Gannen studied him for a moment, then looked at his brother again. "Let's try this then," Gannen said. "R.V. and Steve Leonard are close friends. Leonard designed R.V.'s hooks and persuaded us to blood him. I don't think R.V. would kill the woman if it meant Leonard's death, despite his threats. When you leave, you can take Leonard with you. If you escape, perhaps you'll be able to use him to bargain for the woman's life at a later time." He squinted at me warningly. "That is the best I can do — and it's more than you have a right to expect."

I thought it over, realized this was Debbie's only real hope, and nodded imperceptibly.

"Is that a yes?" Gannen asked.

"Yes," I croaked.

"Then go now!" he snapped. "From the moment you start to walk, the clock begins to tick. In fifteen minutes, we come — and if we catch you, you die."

At a signal from Gannen, the vampaneze and vampets drew back and regrouped around him. Gannen stood in front of them all, hands folded across his chest, waiting for us to leave.

I shuffled forward to my three friends, pushing Steve ahead of me. Vancha still had hold of his captured vampet and was gripping him as I gripped Steve. "Is he serious?" I asked in a whisper.

"It seems so," Vancha replied, though I could tell he hardly believed it either.

"Why is he doing this?" Mr Crepsley asked. "He knows it is our mission to kill the Lord of the Vampaneze. By offering us this opportunity, he frees us to perhaps recover and strike again."

"It's crazy," Vancha agreed, "but we'd be just as crazy to look this gift horse in the mouth. Let's get out before he changes his mind. We can debate it later — if we survive."

Keeping his vampet in front of him, as a shield, Vancha retreated. I followed, an arm wrapped around Steve, who was fully conscious now, but too groggy to make a break for freedom. Mr Crepsley and Harkat came after us. The vampaneze and vampets watched us leave. Many of the red or red-rimmed eyes were filled with loathing and disgust — but none pursued us.

We backed up through the tunnel for a while, until we were certain we weren't being followed. Then we stopped and exchanged uncertain looks. I opened my mouth to say something, but Vancha silenced me before I spoke. "Let's not waste time." Turning, he pushed his vampet ahead of him and began jogging. Harkat took off after him, shrugging helplessly at me as he passed. Mr Crepsley pointed at me to go next, with Steve. Shoving Steve in front, I poked him in the back with the tip of my sword, and roughly encouraged him forward at a brisk pace.

Up through the long, dark tunnels we padded, the hunters and their prisoners, beaten, bloodied, bruised and bewildered. I thought about the Vampaneze Lord, the insane R.V. and his hapless prisoner — Debbie. It tore me up inside to leave her behind, but I had no choice. Later, if I lived, I'd return for her. Right now I had to think only of my own life.

With a great effort, I thrust all thoughts of Debbie from my head and concentrated on the path ahead. At the back of my mind, unbidden, a clock formed, and with every footstep I could hear the hands ticking down the seconds, cutting away at our period of grace, bringing us relentlessly closer to the moment when Gannen Harst would set the vampaneze and vampets after us — freeing the hounds of hell.

TO BE CONTINUED...

WILL THE HUNTERS SURVIVE THE NIGHT
OR BECOME VICTIMS OF THE

KILLERS OF THE DAWN

A STRONG spotlight was trained on the window to dazzle us. Retreating, Vancha cursed his vilest, while the rest of us glanced uneasily at one another, waiting for someone to propose a plan.

A voice from outside, amplified by a megaphone, cut our thoughts short. "You in there!" it bellowed. "*Killers!*"

Vancha hurried to the window and nudged the blind aside a fraction. Light from the sun and spotlight flooded the room. Letting the blind fall back into place, Vancha roared, "Turn off the light!"

"Not a chance!" the person with the megaphone laughed in reply.

Vancha stood there a moment, thinking, then nodded at Mr Crepsley and Harkat. "Check the corridors above and below. Find out if they're inside the building. Don't bait them — if that lot outside start firing, they'll cut us to ribbons."

Mr Crepsley and Harkat obeyed without question and returned within a minute.

"They're packed tight two floors ... above," Harkat reported.

"The same two floors below," Mr Crepsley said grimly.

"Then we have to talk to them," Vancha said. "Find out where we stand and maybe buy some time to think this through. Anyone want to volunteer?" Nobody replied. "Guess that means I'm the negotiator. Just don't blame me if it all goes wrong." Leaving the blind over the window, he shouted at the humans below. "Who's down there and what do you want?"

There was a pause, then the same voice as before spoke to us via a megaphone. "Who am I talking to?" the person asked. Now that I concentrated on the voice, I realized it was a woman's.

"None of your business!" Vancha roared.

Another pause. Then, "We know your names. Larten Crepsley, Vancha March, Darren Shan and Harkat Mulds. I just want to know which one of you I'm in contact with."

Vancha's jaw dropped.

"Tell them who you are," Harkat whispered. "They know too much. Best to act like we're ... co-operating."

Vancha nodded, then shouted through the covered hole in the window, "Vancha March."

"Listen, March," the woman called out. "I'm Chief Inspector Alice Burgess. I'm running this freak show." An ironic choice of words, though none of us commented on it. "If you want to negotiate a deal, you'll be negotiating with me. One warning — I'm not here to play games. I've two hundred men and women out here and inside your building, just dying to put a round of bullets through your hearts. At the first sign that you're messing with us, I'll give the order and they'll open fire. Understand?"

Vancha bared his teeth and snarled, "I understand."

"OK," Chief Inspector Burgess responded. "This is how it works. Come down, one at a time. Any sign of a weapon, or any unexpected moves, and you're history."

"Let's talk about this," Vancha shouted.

A rifle fired and a volley of bullets tore up the outside of the building. We fell to the floor, cursing and yelping, although there was no cause for concern — the marksmen were aiming deliberately high.

When the screams of the bullets died away, the Chief Inspector addressed us again. "That was a warning — your last. Next time we shoot to kill. No talking or bargaining. One minute — then we come in after you."

A troubling silence descended.

"That's that," Harkat muttered after a handful of slow-ticking seconds. "We're finished."

"Not necessarily," Mr Crepsley said softly. "There *is* a way out."

"How?" Vancha asked.

"The window," Mr Crepsley said. "We jump. They will not expect that."

Vancha considered the plan. "The drop's no problem," he mused. "But what do we do once down there?"

"We flit," Mr Crepsley said. "I will carry Darren. You can carry Harkat. It will not be easy – they might shoot us before we work up to flitting speed – but it can be done. With luck."

"It's crazy," Vancha growled, then winked at us. "I like it!"

"Time's up!" Alice Burgess shouted through her megaphone. "Come out immediately or we open fire!"

Vancha grunted, checked his shuriken belts and wrapped his animal hides tight around him. "Ready?" he asked.

"Ready," we said.

"Harkat jumps with me," Vancha said. "Larten and Darren — you come next. Give us a second or two to roll out of your way."

"Luck, Vancha," Mr Crepsley said.

"Luck," Vancha replied, then grinned savagely, slapped Harkat on the back, and leapt through the window, shattering the blind, Harkat not far behind. Mr Crepsley and I waited the agreed seconds, then jumped through the jagged remains of the window after our friends, and dropped swiftly to the ground like a couple of wingless bats, into the hellish cauldron which awaited us below.